CHASING HADLEY

(THE HONEYTON MYSTERIES, BOOK 1)

JESSICA SORENSEN

Chasing Hadley
Jessica Sorensen
All rights reserved.
Copyright © 2018 by Jessica Sorensen
This is a work of fiction. Any resemblance of characters to actual persons, living or dead, is purely coincidental. The author holds exclusive rights to this work. Unauthorized duplication is prohibited. No part of this book can be reproduced in any form or by electronic or mechanical means including information storage and retrieval systems, without the permission in writing from the author. The only exception is by a reviewer who may quote short excerpts in a review.
Any trademarks, service marks, product names or names featured are assumed to be the property of their respective owners, and are used only for reference. There is no implied endorsement if we use one of these terms.

ISBN: 9781939045430

For information: jessicasorensen.com
Cover Design by Mae I Design

❀ Created with Vellum

My family has moved a total of fifteen times in my almost eighteen years of existence. That's almost one move per year. Up until I was ten, though, we lived in the same two-story townhome in the middle of a quaint neighborhood, so technically, we've moved almost two times a year.

I hate moving. Let's get that right out of the way. I hate packing up all my stuff into boxes, the taping, the labeling—all the work. And then, usually only days later, when we've arrived at our new home, the process happens again, only backward. It's exhausting, especially since I'm the one who unpacks most of the boxes. I'm not even sure how I got stuck with the job. How my three younger sisters decided they'd only unpack their own shit, while I unpack my stuff, the kitchen, the living room, the bathroom, and ... well, you get the picture.

I guess, since I'm basically in charge of our household these days, it sort of makes sense.

After our mom died eight years ago, being the oldest and most responsible in the house, the job fell on me. Even my dad relies on me to take care of everything. Like, for instance, now.

The trailer attached to his beat-up pickup is crammed with all our belongings. Boxes are also piled into the bed and back seat of the truck, and the trunk of my 1969 Chevelle is filled with to the brim, as well.

The house we just moved out of—a singlewide with a field of dead grass surrounding it—is all cleaned out, thanks to me and Londyn, one of my sisters. We pulled an all-nighter last night, wanting everything ready to go so we could get an early start, since Honeyton, the small town we're moving to, is about an eight-hour drive from here. I took a powernap at around five o'clock, and then woke everyone up at seven. It's now eight thirty. We should be on the road by now, but my dad can't find his damn car keys.

Of course.

He's constantly losing or misplacing his stuff—it's one of the few things he's consistent with anymore.

Well, that, getting fired, and getting drunk. I blame most of his scatterbrained tendencies on the booze.

Before he started drinking, he was more responsible, involved, a proud father who worked as an undercover detective. Now he can barely remember to take a shower, sometimes going weeks on end without one, which can get really smelly. He's unemployed more than he's employed and works jobs that would make the old him cringe. Currently, he's between jobs, hence the reason we're moving. After getting fired from his position at a plumbing store for showing up drunk, he spent three months straight hanging out at the bar almost every single day and night. He blew all our rent money on drinks, including what my sisters and I had saved up from our random jobs.

A month ago, an eviction notice was stuck to the door. None of us were surprised. It's become a routine. We get evicted, and Dad gets a reality check for a couple weeks where he eases off the drinking and finds us a new place to live, sometimes in the same town, sometimes not. Then we all pack up our shit, which isn't a lot of stuff—moving so much has made us become minimalists, and we don't have a lot of extra cash to buy a ton of crap—and hit the road. After we get moved in to the new place, Dad finds a job, and a few weeks in, he starts drinking again.

That is the Harlyton routine. And yes, it's about as

sucky as it sounds, but we do what we must to make the best of a shitty situation.

I have my own plans, though. Get good grades, stay out of trouble … when I can, and make sure my sisters do, too. Once I graduate, I'm hightailing it to college. I don't even care where. I just want to go someplace where I can stay put for a few years and obtain some structure like I used to have before my mom passed away.

"Did you leave them at the bar last night?" I ask my dad as I circle his truck, searching for his car keys.

We've spent the last twenty minutes looking for them to no avail. He can't even remember the last time he had or used them since he walks to and from the bar.

He pats the pockets of his jacket with a crinkle forming between his brows. "I don't think so." He presses his lips together as he studies me. "You didn't by chance touch them yesterday, did you?"

I shake my head, more than annoyed. He's constantly blaming me for breaking things, losing things, the power getting turned off, the car breaking down—stupid shit. He thinks everything is my responsibility. And it always ends up being his fault, either because he's drunk off his ass, spent the bill money on booze, or didn't keep up with the maintenance on his truck.

"No," I reply in a clipped tone.

Sighing, he digs his phone out of his pocket. "Let me call Larry and see if they're at the bar by chance."

Good old Larry, the owner of the corner bar where Dad likes to spend most of his time. The guy also drinks as much as Dad does, so there's a fat chance in stupid drunkenville that Larry's going to have a clue where the keys are.

"All right, you do that." I back toward the house. "Londyn, Bailey, Payton, and I will search the house again."

I motion for my sisters to follow me inside, earning a scowl from Payton and a glare from Bailey, the two youngest of the Harlyton sisters, with me being the oldest. Londyn is only a year younger than me and will be turning seventeen next month. Bailey and Payton are twins, not identical, and will be celebrating their sixteenth birthday only a week after Londyn's birthday. My parents had us really close on purpose, or so they used to say whenever they'd reminisce. They also wanted a son, but after having the twins, they decided four daughters was enough. Although, our dad used to often joke that they should've tried for more.

He doesn't joke about that anymore. Doesn't joke about much of anything since our mom passed away.

"Why is he always losing shit?" Bailey gripes as the four of us drag our butts inside the empty trailer.

It's the end of summer, and with the windows

closed, the air is stifling hot and muggy, like the air outside. I'm not a fan of the intense heat, but harsh winters suck balls, too. According to the online city page, Honeyton has mild summers and winters, so I guess that's good. Although, the small town is out in the middle of nowhere with no close cities nearby, so that's going to suck.

"Because he's drunk all the time and doesn't give a shit about anything," Payton mutters as she leans against the wall, texting on her old-school, hand-me-down phone.

Sighing, I take the phone from her. "Help find the keys so we can get going. You can have this back when we do." I pocket her phone. "The sun's already going to be setting by the time we get there, and I hate moving in when it's dark."

"Dad probably didn't even call to get the power turned on," Bailey mumbles as she peers inside a drawer.

"No, he didn't." I start opening drawers, too. "I did."

Londyn sighs as she opens a window. "Of course you did."

I frown at her. "What's that tone supposed to mean?"

She fans her hand in front of her face, trying to cool off. "It means you always do everything."

I cross my arms. "You say that like it's a bad thing."

"It is, and it isn't. I mean … don't you ever get tired of doing all this crap all the time?" She tucks a strand of her shoulder-length brown hair behind her ear. "He's supposed to be the adult, yet we're the ones getting the power turned on, trying to keep up with the bills, and trying to figure out where the hell he put his car keys after he stumbles home drunk at three in the morning. And he didn't even bother helping us finish packing, even when he saw we were still up."

"He may have not noticed," I point out, not really trying to defend him, just stating the sad obvious. "He was pretty trashed."

"And he's super hungover today," Bailey adds as she opens the small pantry closet. "I caught him throwing up in the neighbors' bushes earlier."

I crinkle my nose. "Did you clean it up?"

"Fuck no." She slams the cupboard door. "I know you think it's your job to clean up his messes, but I don't want any part of it." She wanders toward the hall-way, mumbling, "I'm the child, and he's supposed to be the parent. Not the other way around."

I sigh heavily. Out of the three of us, Bailey has the hardest time. She's also been going through a serious emo phase lately, refusing to wear anything but black, and she is always moody. Her outlet is usually music. She spends hours blasting songs while singing and playing along on her guitar. She even writes her own music.

The problem is, about three months ago, our house got broken into. I wasn't really surprised, considering the type of neighborhood we live in. However, Bailey's guitar, amp, and her stereo system were all taken—stuff she had before our mom passed away. It was the only stuff of value she owned, and the guitar held sentimental value. We spent days searching pawnshops, secondhand stores, and asking around, seeing if we could find them to no avail. She's been in a foul mood ever since.

"We should really find a way to come up with some extra cash, so we can buy her a new guitar," Londyn says as she leans against the counter. "Maybe that'll pull her out of her funk."

I lie flat on the floor to look underneath the fridge for the keys. "I wish we had some extra cash, but I already had to sell some of Mom's old jewelry so we could pay the deposits and stuff on the new house."

"You did what?" Payton reels toward me, slamming a cupboard door.

I push up from the floor and dust off my hands. "It's not like I wanted to, but we needed the money, and it's the only thing of real value I could find to pawn."

"I don't give a shit why you did it. Mom left that jewelry to all of us, not just you." Payton storms out of the room in the direction Bailey took off in. I'm sure she's going to inform her of how badly she thinks I fucked up.

By the time we get in the car to hit the road, the two of them will be pissed off at me and giving me the silent treatment, which isn't always a punishment, despite what they think. Still, it doesn't make me feel any less guilty for pawning off some of our mom's necklaces and bracelets, but I had no other choice. I wish they would try to understand that.

"Did you get rid of her wedding ring?" Londyn asks quietly, tracing her fingertip over her ring finger.

"No, I just got rid of a couple necklaces and bracelets that she rarely wore." I take a deep breath as tears sting my eyes. "I'd never get rid of her wedding ring, no matter how hard up for cash we are."

She nods, lifting her gaze from her finger. "I'm sorry."

"For what?"

"That you have to make these decisions." She smiles sadly then gives me a hug.

I hug her back, letting myself have a moment to be needy.

Out of my three sisters, I'm closest with Londyn, since we're barely a year apart. Bailey and Payton are twins, so they've always paired up with each other. But Londyn and I don't share too much in common, except for the fact that we're tough as shit—all the Harlyton sisters are. Where Londyn is more quiet and reserved, I tend to be a bit loud and complicated. Not always intentionally. Most of my complications are just piled on me. And like I said earlier, one day I'm going to live a simple, structured life.

Our personalities aren't the only trait that's different. Londyn likes to rock the simple jeans, T-shirts, and Converse sneakers look; her hair is always down and straight; and she almost never wears makeup. Me, I've got the whole alternative, edgy thing going on. My wavy brown hair is swept to the side with tiny, woven braids on one side. Right now, I have on a black T-shirt, cut-offs, and a plaid shirt tied around my waist. My clunky boots are unlaced, several rings cover my fingers, a series of leather bands decorate my wrists, and my ears are ornamented with stud and looped earrings. Kohl eyeliner is my trademark look, along with lip gloss. I don't have any tattoos, but I plan on getting one as soon as Payton masters the art, which is a goal of hers.

"Thanks, I needed that," I say as Londyn pulls back from the hug.

"I could tell." She gives a quick glance around the living room. "You know, it's strange, but I don't even get sad about moving anymore. I don't think I'm even going to miss this place."

"Me either." It's the truth. We didn't live here long enough to tie ourselves to anything. Plus, we've gotten into the habit of not getting attached, not getting too close to the friends we make, or to the homes we live in. After the fourth move, we realized doing so only made moving harder, so we put up walls around ourselves, only letting each other in. Because, when it all comes down to it, my sisters are the only constants in my life, no matter how much we fight or wear on each other's nerves.

Taking a final look around at the shaggy brown carpet, the bare walls, and the outdated kitchen, I sigh, ready to say goodbye to this place and get on the road.

"You know what? If Larry doesn't know where his keys are, I say we just hotwire his truck," I tell Londyn as I reach to close the window she opened earlier.

She nods. "I'm cool with that, but Dad might have a shitfit."

"I really don't care. It's his own damn fault for getting shit-faced the night before we move then misplacing his keys."

"I completely agree."

Silence encases us, except for the soft chatter of Bailey and Payton floating from the other side of their shut bedroom door.

"I miss who he used to be," Londyn whispers suddenly. "I wish we had our old dad back."

So do I, Londyn, so do I.

I don't say the words aloud. No, I learned a long time ago, the day our mom passed away to be exact, that wishing is just a waste of time. That was the last day I stopped believing in wishes.

That was the day I stopped believing in a lot of things.

CHAPTER TWO

LARRY DOESN'T HAVE THE CAR KEYS, SO WE END UP hotwiring Dad's truck while he's distracted with vomiting in the neighbors' bushes again. Or, well, *I* hotwire his truck.

Cars are sort of my thing. Always have been. My first word was *race*. That was my mom's doing. She chanted the word repeatedly until I said it.

She was really into cars and racing. She even went professional for a while before she got pregnant with me and married my dad. That still didn't stop her from racing locally. One of my first memories was when I was about three or four, and I went to watch her race on the back streets of town. I was the only kid there, and that made me feel super special. But not as special as I felt when my mom won the race. My dad was so happy that he took her out to dinner to celebrate. He bought her a necklace beforehand to give her as a prize for winning. At the time, I couldn't figure out how my dad knew she was going to win. Later, I realized he didn't really know. He just hoped. And if she hadn't won, he still would've given her that necklace.

I remember how happy she was when he gave it to her, the way her eyes lit up. That necklace was one of the pieces of jewelry I had to pawn the other day. I asked my dad beforehand if it was okay. He said he didn't give a shit, then took off to the bar.

Life is so fucked up. Sometimes, I can't even stand it. But I'll never admit that aloud, being the glue that holds this family together. Although, I sometimes feel like the really shitty, cheap kind of glue.

After I hotwire Dad's truck, he briefly bitches me out for doing so before climbing in. He looks awful— pale skin, bags under his bloodshot eyes, and he smells like a guy who spent all night doing shots of whiskey with his buddies at the local bar, which is exactly what he did.

"You think he'll be okay to drive?" Londyn asks as the four of us pile into my Chevelle. "He's super hungover."

Payton and Bailey slide into the back seat, and Bailey instantly rests her head against the window and shuts her eyes, refusing to speak to me.

"I tried to convince him to let me drive his truck, and you could drive my car, but he's in one of his asshole moods." I shut the door and turn on the ignition, firing up the engine.

While my car needs some bodywork, the engine is in excellent shape. It was actually a project car my mom and I were working on before she passed away. It was supposed to be finished a long time ago, but without much extra money or time, I haven't been able to work on it as much as I want to.

"So, a normal mood then," Payton grumbles, resting back in the seat.

Bailey snickers while I sigh, knowing they're right. More often than not, our dad is an asshole.

"I say we follow him for an hour or so," I suggest. "And then, if he looks like he's struggling, we'll say we need to make a pit stop, and then I'll make him let me drive."

"And how are you going to do that?" Londyn fastens her seatbelt. "You know how stubborn he can get."

I smile wickedly. "I'll un-hotwire it and refuse to start it up again until he agrees."

She only frowns. "What if he throws a fit? I hate when he does that, especially when we're in a public place."

True. Our dad can throw the biggest tantrums. He didn't used to be like that. I think all the drinking makes him temperamental or, well, when he has to stop drinking. And since he's sober right now … well, there's a good chance he's going to cause a scene if we try to say he can't drive.

Still …

"I'll handle his temper tantrum. It's better than letting him drive when he's too tired." I put my own seatbelt on then back out of the driveway.

"I wish he'd stop acting like a child." Londyn stares out the window.

I really hope she stops wishing so much. Maybe then she wouldn't seem so disappointed all the time. I'm not about to tell her that, though.

The four of us sink into silence as I pull out onto the dusty road and follow our dad's truck toward the main part of town. Halfway there, Payton asks for her phone, and I hand it to her after she promises to behave. Then we're all quiet again, the music from the stereo filling up the silence. It's not our usual MO to be so quiet. Maybe it's the whole silent treatment thing, or perhaps we're all just fed-up with moving and are sinking into our own depressed thoughts.

Sure, this town was shitty and the trailer we lived in smelled like skunk half the damn time, thanks to a skunk spraying it while it camped out underneath the trailer, but I'm sure the place we're going to won't be any better. It will be just as rundown, and more than likely, we'll be doing this same thing six months from now. When I really analyze it, everything feels so hopeless, which is why I never try to analyze it.

Shit. I need to get everyone out of their own heads.

I start to suggest we play a road game, when Bailey lets out a heart-skipping squeal.

"What the hell?" Payton says, nearly jolting out of her skin.

Londyn jerks, too, her eyes blinking wildly.

"My guitar!" Bailey shouts, pointing out the window at the local pawnshop on the corner of Main Street. "That's my guitar in there." She pats the back of my seat. "Hadley, stop the car."

I pull over at the curb in front of the store and shove the shifter into park. Sure enough, positioned in a stand in front of the shop's window is Bailey's guitar. I know that for a fact because she had Payton paint her initials on the front in fancy script.

"We have to go in and get it, Hadley." She pushes on the back of my seat. "Come on, let's go before someone goes in and buys it."

I internally grimace. If the shop is selling the guitar for more than ten bucks, which I'm sure it is, I won't be able to buy it for her.

I trade a worried glance with Londyn before getting out. Bailey immediately jumps out, and Payton puts her phone away and runs after her. The two of them hurry inside, Londyn and I slowly trailing after them.

"What're you going to do?" she whispers as I open the door. "We can't afford to buy it."

"I'm not sure yet." I send our dad a text that we had to pull over and that he should stop at the gas station at the edge of town and wait for us. When he doesn't respond right away, I worry he may have lost his phone, too.

Lovely.

A frown forms at her lips. "Don't do anything stupid."

I stuff my phone into the back pocket of my shorts. "Like what?"

"Like give something up to get her guitar."

"I don't even have anything to give up."

She gives me a pressing look. "That's because you already gave everything up."

I mirror her look. "Then I guess we don't really have a problem."

She sighs before walking over to the glass countertops that are filled with old jewelry. I make my way over to the window where Bailey is scooping up her guitar and Payton is sifting through a stack of paintings.

"It's mine for sure," Bailey announces as she strums the strings. "See? My initials are on the front."

"Yeah, I see them." I swallow hard as I note the price tag.

One hundred freakin' bucks.

Shit, shit, shit, double shit.

Bailey plucks a couple of chords as she hops down from the window, ready to go, but I stop her before she walks out the door.

"You can't just take it, Bay," I say with a bit of remorse.

"Why not? It's mine." She hugs the guitar to her chest. "For all we know, the shop owner was the one who stole it."

Doubtful. And even if they did, there's still not much we can do about it, except go to the police. But considering they weren't very helpful when our trailer was broken into, I doubt they're going to be much help with this.

Back in the day, our dad would have known what to do, since he used to work as a detective. Now he rarely helps us out, especially with anything related to the past. Plus, he also hasn't replied to the text I sent him earlier, so who the hell even knows where he is right now.

"Can I help you?" The store owner, a fifty-something-year-old guy with thinning hair and wearing a floral, button down shirt and board shorts emerges from the back room. He eyeballs us warily, then his gaze zones in on Bailey. "No touching the merchandise unless you plan on buying it." He points to a sign hanging behind the counter that basically states what he just told us.

I open my mouth to say, well, I'm not sure yet, but Bailey speaks first.

"We don't need to buy this. It belongs to me. You stole it." She lifts her chin and gives the store owner a defiant look.

The store owner rolls his eyes. "Yeah, like I haven't heard that before."

"It's true." Bailey steps toward him, flipping her long, brown hair off her shoulder. "It was stolen from me a few months ago. I think you already know that, though."

"I'm not a thief, so shut your trap, kid. That guitar was brought in here, and I gave the person cash for it." He crosses the room, pushing past me, and reaches to take the guitar from Bailey. "I don't steal things."

Bailey's nostrils flare. and her hands curl into fists. While I'm not straight-up sure if she'll punch the store owner dude, she has been known to get into a few brawls and was even arrested for one once.

Not wanting to go down that road again, I jump between them, facing the store owner with my arms crossed. "Look, I don't think you're a thief, but what I do know is that guitar is hers. Someone stole it from our house, and now it's here. We'd really like it back, so if you could help us out, I'd greatly appreciate it." My tone comes out firm but polite. I hope it'll be enough to win him over. I'm not holding my breath, though. This guy seems like a straight-up douchebag.

"Yeah, I can help you out." He leans in, and I try not to cringe at the foul, rotten egg stench emitting from his breath. "Give me two hundred bucks and the guitar's yours."

I open and flex my fingers. "The price tag says one hundred."

"Yeah, and I'm adding on a fee." He smirks. "For having to deal with this shit."

I grit my teeth. *I will not hit an old dude. I will not hit an old dude.* "That's called false advertisement."

"So? What're you going to do about it?" He folds his arms, his smirk growing.

"I could report you," I say. "I highly doubt that guitar is the one thing you've got in here that's stolen."

He lifts his shoulders. "Go ahead. Report me. Like I give a shit." He casually leans against the counter, as if he has all the time in the world. "Newsflash, sweetheart, we live in one of the trashiest, higher crime towns in the state. No one gives a rat's ass whether I sell stolen goods or not. The police have way bigger problems to worry about."

Fuck, he's right, but that doesn't mean I'm going to let him charge us two hundred dollars for the guitar.

"I'll give you eighty bucks for it," I say, and Londyn shakes her head.

"Two hundred and fifty," he counters with that stupid smirk.

I usually try to avoid fights, but this dude seriously needs to get punched in the face.

He must see the urge written all over my expression and in the twitch of my hand, because he says, "Go ahead and hit me. Like I fucking care. It'll be like getting hit by a kitten."

He may say that now, but he hasn't been punched by a Harlyton sister before. Sure, we may not look tough—our builds are tall and slightly gangly—but that doesn't mean we don't know how to throw down a proper punch.

We all started taking self-defense and kickboxing classes the moment our dad first made us move, and we learned how to toughen up quickly. The first move was only a couple months after our mom died when Dad sold the house because, according to him, we needed a fresh start. Apparently, that fresh start meant moving into a rundown house in the middle of the sketchiest area of the city where robberies, drug dealings, and every illegal activity imaginable took place. When I asked my dad why we couldn't rent a place in a better area, he told me we couldn't afford it. It made no sense —still doesn't—since he made a decent profit off our house. What he did with the money is beyond me, since he refuses to tell us.

Anyway, as much as I want to punch this shithead store owner in the face, we're pressed for time.

"Can you take Bailey and Payton out to the car?" I ask Londyn, gently prying the guitar away from Bailey.

Londyn's gaze flicks between the store owner to me. "I'd rather not leave you alone with Creepy Creeperson over here."

"Who the hell are you calling creepy?" The store owner glares at her.

"You, obviously, since I'm staring right at you," Londyn quips with a smirk.

She rarely gets this sassy. I think I might be wearing on her, or maybe the move is.

"I'll be fine," I assure Londyn when the store owner's face starts to turn bright red. "You can wait right outside the door if you want to. I just need to talk to him for a moment."

Shaking her head, she walks by me and signals for Bailey and Payton to follow. Payton briskly strolls out of the store, making me wonder what the hell she's up to, whereas Bailey refuses to budge.

"I'm not leaving without my guitar." She folds her arms and gives me a defiant look.

I lower my voice. "I'm going to get the guitar, but I need to make a bargain with this guy, and it'll be easier if you're not in here, okay?"

Her gaze drops to the guitar then back up to my face. "You swear you won't walk out of here without it?"

"I swear to the moon and back," I utter the words our mom used to whisper whenever she made an unbreakable promise.

With a small nod, Bailey walks away, giving me one final glance before pushing out the door.

Letting a slow exhale ease from my lips, I face douchebag McGee. "All right, here's the deal. I don't have two hundred and fifty bucks on me, nor am I planning on giving you that much cash for something that's worth about a hundred bucks." I don't bother mentioning the sentimental value is worth way more than that. He'd just use that against me. "I will, however, give you this in exchange." Gently setting the guitar down, I fumble as I reach up and unclasp the necklace hanging around my neck.

On the end of the chain is a silver heart-shaped locket that has a small diamond in the center. My mom gave it to me for my ninth birthday. She said her mom gave it to her when she turned that age. It's not extremely valuable in terms of dollars, but it's priceless to me.

"I'm sure you can get at least two hundred bucks for it." I hold up the necklace for him to see.

He squints at the locket. "Is that a real diamond?"

"Yeah," I manage to say in an even voice.

"Hmmm …" He runs his finger along the diamond before looking back at me. "I'll give you fifty bucks for it."

I clutch the chain. "You'll give me the guitar for it. And I know you will because the necklace is worth more."

He studies me for a moment before he snatches the necklace from my hand then rounds behind the counter. "I'm going to make sure it's a real diamond before I make the trade."

"Sounds good." I lean against the counter and wait, tears burning my eyes. I suck them back, knowing if I ever let those tears out, I'll probably drown in them.

TEN MINUTES LATER, I'M CLIMBING INTO THE CHEVELLE with Bailey's guitar, feeling pretty shitty about the whole necklace exchange. But when Bailey's eyes light up for the first time in months, it makes me feel a bit better.

"Thank you, Hadley." Bailey leans over the seat and gives me a hug. "You're the best big sister ever."

I hug her back, ignoring Londyn's accusing gaze boring into me. "You're welcome. I just want you to be happy."

"I am right now. I promise." She gives me one final hug before sitting back in the seat and plucking the strings.

"Your necklace is missing," Londyn mutters under her breath as I start the engine.

"I packed it up. Didn't want to risk losing it while we were hauling out boxes. You know how I'm always losing things." I shift the car into drive.

She rolls her eyes. "Sure you did."

I just shrug and steer out onto the road. She may be upset with me now, but she'll get over it. She always does.

Silence stretches between us as I drive toward the gas station, hoping Dad is waiting for us there. Since he hasn't texted me back yet, I'm feeling pretty doubtful.

"That guy was a real asshole, wasn't he?" Londyn absentmindedly twists a ring on her finger.

"Yes, he was," I agree, cracking my window. "I seriously about punched that smirk right off his face."

"You should've." She slips off her sneakers and props her feet on the dashboard.

"Since when do you encourage fighting?" I question.

She shrugs. "You're my sister, and he was trying to

take advantage of you. He needed a good punch in the face."

I can't help smiling as I slip on my sunglasses. Londyn rarely encourages drama, so that store owner must have really gotten under her skin.

"If it makes you guys feel any better, I totally jacked an art set from him," Payton announces from the back seat.

Londyn and I trade a confused look before glancing back at her.

She smiles wickedly as she holds up a flat, wooden box in her hand. "It hasn't even been opened yet."

So that's why she hauled ass out of the store.

I really should reprimand her for stealing—she's already a borderline klepto—but, since I just paid for a guitar that was stolen from us, I think I'll let this one slide. Plus, it's not like none of us steal. We've all done it before in desperate times.

"What's in it?" I ask as I turn into the gas station parking lot.

Shit, I don't see our dad's truck anywhere.

"It says it's got pencils and paints," Payton tells me. "Which I'm in desperate need of."

I nod distractedly as I make a loop around the gas station.

"Why are we here?" Londyn asks, rolling her window down all the way.

"I texted Dad when we stopped at the pawn shop and told him to wait for us here." I frown as I realize his truck isn't here. "I guess he didn't get the message."

"Or ignored it," Londyn gripes in frustration. "Why does he have to make everything such a pain in the ass?"

Because he misses Mom. Because he's depressed. Because he's heartbroken.

Those are the excuses I usually make for him, but I'm getting tired of it. I understand that he misses her, that he loved her more than he loved himself. She made him happy, and he thrived on making her happy.

Watching the two of them together was like witnessing magic. I don't even care how cheesy that makes me sound. I've never seen any other couple have such love glowing in their eyes as when Mom and Dad looked at each other adoringly. I used to want that for myself, that magic and the glowing. After watching the absence of it smother my dad in darkness, though, I changed my mind. It's part of why I don't do the whole dating thing. Why I've kissed a total of two guys, and one was on a dare; the other was a drunken mistake. And I have no plans of upping that number anytime soon. Life is easier that way.

Relationships are complicated. And complications are distracting. Which brings me to the other part of the reason I don't date.

I don't want anything distracting me from my goals of escaping this life. I'm going to college the moment I'm handed my diploma, and I don't need anything or anyone holding me back. It's already going to be hard enough saying goodbye to my sisters.

"Should we go look for him?" Londyn asks right as my phone vibrates from inside my pocket.

"Hold that thought." I fish out my phone, crossing my fingers the message is from our dad, telling me he's parked somewhere in town, waiting for us.

But he can never make things that easy, can he?

Dad: Just got your message. I'm about to pull into that bar just outside of town on the highway. Meet me there when you're ready.

"Oh, hell no." I strap my seatbelt on and tell my sisters to do the same, knowing if he steps foot in that bar, he won't be coming out anytime soon, unless I drag his drunk-ass out.

None of my sisters even bother asking me what's wrong—our dad is super predictable these days. They simply put on their seatbelts then hold on, knowing they're going to need to. Because, if there's one thing I'm good at in this life, it's driving fast.

Moments later, I'm peeling out with the gas pedal floored. My heart is pumping as the speed increases. I feel more alive than I have in weeks.

My mom used to say the same thing, that racing

made her breathe freer and her heart beat swifter. She enjoyed every moment she spent behind the wheel. I've been the same way from the moment I started learning how to drive, back when I was ten. Mom let me sit on her lap and steer down our driveway. It was such a rush, and I couldn't wait until I got my learner's permit. Although, by the time I did, she was gone, but the magic I experienced the first time sparkled just as brightly.

Driving has always given me a rush, and when I'm racing, all the shit going on in my life sort of blurs away. Unfortunately, I don't get to race very often since I have to be sneaky about it. Because, while my dad is a mess and barely pays attention to us anymore, he did set one firm rule.

Absolutely no drag racing.

I understand why he thinks we need the rule, since Mom died racing when her car skidded off the road and into a lake. I was there when it happened. To this day, I still remember the sounds of the tires skidding and the splash. I don't remember much after that, except a scream. My memory is blank of the following days until her funeral, as if my mind wiped the days clean.

A lot of people tried to get my dad to put me in therapy, saying the trauma probably gave me selective amnesia, but he was too engulfed in his own sorrow to follow through with the suggestions. So, we had the funeral, said our goodbyes, and all tried to move on with our lives. But my heart constantly feels broken. And that's during the day. At night, I'm haunted by nightmares of what little I can remember.

The only time my heart doesn't feel broken is when I'm racing. That's what my dad doesn't understand—that I need to race to keep floating in this shitty pool of muddy, scummy pond water that I'm struggling to keep afloat in. Racing is my only breath of fresh air, my passion, and I'm damn good at it, something I more than prove when I skid into the parking lot of the bar right as our dad is about to walk inside.

A cloud of dirt kicks up and gusts into the rolled down windows of my car and around my dad as I brake hard. He gapes at us in shock. Then the moment the surprise wears off, sheer lividness flashes across his face as he strides toward the car. I know what's coming next. He's going to yell at me, make a scene, threaten to take away my car keys. Wouldn't be the first time.

"Give me your fucking car keys. Now!" he seethes as he reaches my door.

"No—" I start, but he reaches in, shuts off the engine, and steals my keys. "Hey." I move to snatch them from him, but he stuffs them into his pocket and strides away toward the bar door.

I dive out of the car and rush after him. "Dad, we

don't have time for this shit. It's already going to be dark by the time we get to Honeyton."

"Well, you should've thought about that before you drove like a goddamn lunatic." He jerks the door to the bar open. "Seriously, what were you thinking? Especially with your sisters in the car."

"I was thinking that I needed to get here before you went inside," I snap. "Because, I knew, if you did, you'd be in there all night and we'd be stuck out in the car, waiting for your drunk-ass to stumble out." This isn't the first time I've lost my cool with him, and it won't be the last.

His face reddens. "I think you're forgetting who the parent is."

"*What parent?*" I'm fuming mad. Mad at him for being a drunk. For being such a shitty father. For pretending he has the right to scold me now when he doesn't give a shit about anything we do. Mad because I had to pawn my necklace. Mad, mad, mad. I'm so mad all the time that I can barely stand it. "Because all I see is a drunk deadbeat who can't even take care of his kids."

He smacks me across the face, shocking both him and me. With all the terrible things my father has done over the years, he has never hit me until now. "I'm sorry," he sputters as I place my palm to my throbbing cheek, my eyes wide. Then he bails into the bar.

Shaking my head, I spin around and storm back to the car. "What a fucking asshole!"

"Holy shit, I can't believe he hit you," Bailey whispers with wide eyes.

Payton's eyes are equally as large, but Londyn appears shockingly pissed off.

"We should leave his ass here." She shakes her head. "Take the truck and ditch him."

The idea does sound enticing, but he's our legal guardian and none of us are eighteen. Even though I hate it, we need him around.

I roll my window down all the way. "We'll give him an hour to cool off, and then I'll go in and get him."

Londyn shakes her head while staring at my cheek. "I can't believe he hit you."

Me neither. And I'm not sure what hurts worse—my face, my pride, or my heart.

CHAPTER THREE

After sitting outside the bar for almost an hour, our dad stumbles out, drunk off his ass. When I refuse to hotwire his truck again, he finally lets Londyn drive his truck. I feel bad for her being stuck in the car with his smelly ass and offer to drive with him instead, but Londyn refuses to allow it. Since my cheek currently has a bright red handprint on it, I don't put up much of an argument.

Five hours into the drive and after Dad sobers up, we pull over and Londyn climbs back into the Chevelle. Everything is going decently until we enter the town of Honeyton, our new, temporary place of residence.

Somewhere along the main street and the turn off to our neighborhood, Dad pulls over. Since we don't notice right away, we're unsure where he went. My bet is the first bar he spotted.

Luckily, I have the new address entered into the GPS on my phone. Unfortunately, I have no clue how the hell we're supposed to get the keys from the landlord, or if Dad's even signed the lease yet. He found the house online, that much I know. Other than that, he hasn't given me any more info other than the address. Not that I haven't tried. He always just dismisses me or gives some vague answer, probably because he's either doing something or has done something I won't approve of.

That's my dad for you.

Yeah, did I forget to mention that he does some pretty shady stuff, pulling off scams and screwing people over? Not that he ever tells me about it. I just hear stuff through gossip or read about it on his police report when I bail him out of jail.

I wonder how long we'll be here before he gets arrested?

Sighing heavily at that thought, I pull up into the gravel driveway of the address currently typed into the GPS. The sun is starting to set, the sky greying. Even if Dad arrives in the next five minutes, we're going to be trying to move stuff in while it's dark.

"Well, I think this one is the winner." Sarcasm drips from Bailey's tone as she takes in the narrow, two-story home in front of us.

The wraparound porch is starting to collapse, the front door is cracked, and one of the windows is boarded up. It does have a garage at the end of the driveway. Or, well, more like a shack with a garage door.

"The winner of what exactly?" Payton slants forward in the back seat to get a better look. "The shittiest house in the neighborhood?"

"Actually, I was going to go with the shittiest house we've ever lived in," Bailey clarifies. "The house next door is much shittier."

Payton's gaze drifts to the two-story home beside ours. It shares similarities to ours, only with more boarded up windows and a shit ton of rusted cars decorating the backyard. Some of the cars don't look half bad, if they had some work done to them.

"Doesn't really matter how shitty it is anyway," Bailey adds as she gathers her guitar and bag. "We'll probably live here for like, what? Maybe six months tops?"

"How did Dad even find this town?" Payton leans back and scribbles something in a notebook. "It's out in the middle of freakin' nowhere. Seriously, did you guys see the population sign?"

"We've lived in small towns before," I remind them as I check my phone for missed messages.

Fuck. He hasn't replied to my texts yet.

Frustrated, I send him another, asking how I'm supposed to get into this place and if he needs to be here to sign a lease. After a couple minutes tick by and he doesn't reply, I shove open the door.

"I'm going to take a look around," I tell my sisters as I hop out of the car.

I hike up the gravel driveway, hoping I can find either a letter from the landlord or an old rental sign that hopefully has a phone number.

The more I walk around, the more my face throbs. I took some painkillers earlier and pressed a cold bottle of soda to my cheek for a while, but it still hurts like a motherfucker and looks just as bad. In a couple days, I'll probably have a bruise.

"Goddamn, stupid, dickless asshole," I chew my dad out as I trot up the steps to the side door.

"Well, hello to you, too."

The voice comes from out of nowhere and startles the crap out of me. I spin around and nearly trip over my untied laces. I grab the wooden railing for support and end up getting slivers in my palms, but at least I manage to stop myself from falling on my ass.

Sweeping my hair out of my face, I glance around to see who the culprit is who almost made me fall on my face. The instant I spot him, I know I'm about to have trouble on my hands.

He's standing on the other side of the fence that

divides the yard between the house next door and ours. He looks around my age, is tall, lean, with blond hair, and one of the prettiest faces I've ever seen. Which yes, is cliché and makes me sound stupidly girlie, but it's the truth. He's also sporting an I-think-I'm-the-shit smirk, or a smirk I like to refer to as "a douchebag stamp."

He rests his arms on top of the fence. "Are you lost, baby?"

My jaw ticks. God, I hate it when guys call me baby.

I cock a brow. "Are you talking to me?"

"Yeah, I am, baby." He deliberately lets his gaze scroll over me before something flashes in his eyes. Perplexity? "Wait. Do I know you?"

I shake my head and roll my eyes. "No. And that line doesn't work on me, dude."

He assesses me with confused interest then plasters on a smirk, cockiness oozing from him once more. "You know what? Forget the baby remark. I'm thinking you're more of a sweetheart sort of girl."

"Oh, my God." I hold up my hands. *I can't even right now.* "Does that shit seriously ever work for you?"

His smile fumbles for the briefest of seconds before he plasters the smirk right back on. "Don't worry; it's okay to be flattered."

"I'm not flattered." I trot down the steps and stop a short distance from him. "But don't worry, *sweetheart;*

I'm sure there's some girl somewhere stupid enough to find your disgusting little obsession with vomit-inducing nicknames swoon-worthy. You should probably go find her, *baby*. And I'm thinking the best place to start is on go-fuck-yourself lane. And don't ever call me sweetheart or baby again or I'll kick you in the dick drive." Then I flip him the middle finger and turn away, heading back down the driveway.

My sisters have gotten out of the car, and Londyn is digging through the trunk while Payton texts on her phone and Bailey watches me with an amused grin.

"Way to make friends with the new neighbors." She gives me a thumbs-up.

"That guy was an ass." I stop in front of her, casting a quick glance back at the guy.

I half expect him to be standing near the fence, glaring at me, but he's walking back to the house. When he reaches the door, he throws a look in my direction, his expression laced with irritation.

"A hot ass," Payton remarks without glancing up from her phone.

Bailey grins as she slings her guitar strap over her shoulder. "For sure."

"Don't." I point a finger back and forth between the two of them. "That isn't the kind of guy you want to date."

"Who said anything about dating?" Payton grins. "Maybe I'm just looking for a boy toy."

Bailey and Payton high-five each other, and I shake my head.

"You're not even sixteen yet. You don't need a boy toy," I lecture. "You should be focused on getting good grades and pursuing your dreams."

"Hooking up with a hottie is on my bucket list," Payton remarks as she shoves her phone into the back pocket of her torn jeans.

I roll my eyes. "That should not be on your bucket list. Cool things should be. Like going to Paris and seeing the ocean. Shit like that."

"That stuff is on my bucket list, too." Payton pulls her curly brown and red streaked hair into a messy bun and secures it with an elastic that's around her wrist. "But hooking up with the hot next-door neighbor is more doable than being able to afford a flight to Paris."

I cross my arms. "With that attitude, you won't."

Payton sighs, tugging on the bottom of her over-sized worn *Nirvana* T-shirt. "You sound like Mom."

Bailey nods. "She really does."

"That's not a bad thing," I utter quietly.

"I didn't mean it as a bad thing." Payton offers me a small smile. "It's just that … Don't you ever get tired of being the responsible one? You're almost eighteen, but sometimes, you act like you're thirty."

"Someone has to be the responsible one," I say, working to keep an even tone to hide the truth. That I do wish I could act my age. But they don't need to know how I feel. Then they'd just feel guilty. "And besides, I don't always act responsible. I do a lot of stupid stuff all the time."

Payton deliberates, nodding. "Yeah, you're probably right. Mom wouldn't have told our next-door neighbor to go fuck himself, and that she was going to kick him in the dick."

"That's not exactly what I said," I argue. "And besides, he deserved it. He was an ass. And you should realize that right now. No flirting with him, okay?"

"We'll see," Payton says with a mischievous glint in her eyes.

Lovely. That more than likely means she's going to go after blondie baby douchebag—my nickname for him from now on. And Bailey will probably flirt with him, too, although she'll back off before Payton does.

Between the two of them, Bailey is more loud and outspoken, except when it comes to guys. Payton is the flirt and has already had her fair share of boyfriends. She assured me a while ago that she is still a virgin, but I still stuffed a cookie jar full of condoms and put it in the bathroom. So far, none of us have used any, but my money is on Payton being the one to stick her hand into that cookie jar first.

"Oh, my God, you're thinking about the condom cookie jar, aren't you?" Payton groans as she heads toward the trunk where Londyn has begun to stack boxes and bags. "Just because we like to talk about sex doesn't mean we're actually having it."

"I know that." I follow her. "But when you do start to be sexually active, I want to make sure you're careful."

"I feel like I'm in health class right now." Payton picks up a box from off the ground. "You want to go get a banana so you can give me a demonstration on how to put one on?"

"That's actually not a bad idea," I joke with a smirk. "But I think a cucumber's closer to the right shape unless his dick is really crooked."

Londyn snickers as she drops a box onto the ground beside her feet. "Like Donny Dapierfield."

I make a face. "Ew. You saw Donny Dapierfield's dick? When?"

"When he took me to prom and asked me to give him a handjob." Her face twists in disgust. "He didn't even wait for me to answer; just pulled out his thing and looked at me expectantly."

I lean against the open trunk. "Please tell me you didn't do it."

"Hell no! I laughed at him. I couldn't help it. His dick

looked like this." She holds up her hand with her index finger curved in.

I snort a laugh. "I would've hit him in his crooked dick and made it even more crooked."

She grabs a bag out of the trunk and sets it on top of a stack of boxes. "I would have, but my laughter must have wounded his ego because he zipped up his pants and drove me straight home without saying another word."

"Um, Hadley," Bailey interrupts. "Where are we supposed to put all these boxes if we can't even get in the house?"

Crap. I almost forgot about the key situation, thanks to blondie baby douchebag distracting me.

"Stack them on the front porch for now. I'm going to take a look around again, without distractions this time, and see if I can figure out how to get ahold of the landlord."

I start up the driveway, sending my dad another text, then go up to the front door and try the knob. It's locked. I have the same luck with the side door, so I start looking around for a sign somewhere, eventually heading over to the shed/garage. The door isn't automatic, and the only way to get in is to push it up by hand. Once I get it open, I feel around for a light switch.

"You shouldn't have done that."

I startle, whirling around toward my neighbors', and

find a girl with light brown, shoulder-length hair, maybe a year or two younger than Bailey and Payton, watching me from the other side of the fence.

That's two times in half an hour that I've been startled by the neighbors, which makes me question if they're going to end up being obnoxious.

"It's okay. I live here," I tell her.

"I didn't mean the garage door." She takes a step toward the fence. "I meant, you shouldn't have said that shit to my brother."

"Who's your brother?" I wonder as I wipe my dusty hands off on the sides of my shorts.

She smiles, but it's more mocking than friendly. "They guy you told to go fuck himself and that you were going to kick in the dick."

"Oh." So, this is blondie baby douchebag's sister. I guess I can kind of see similarities in their features. "That's actually not what I said."

"You sure about that?"

"I just told him the best place to go find a girl who would enjoy his douchebaggery would be on go-fuck-yourself lane and don't ever call me sweetheart or baby again or I'll kick him in the dick drive."

She studies me cautiously. "That's pretty much the same thing."

"Close, but not quite." I move to step into the shed/garage.

"Well, just a little warning," she says, and I pause. "My brothers don't like when one of them gets insulted or hurt, and they'll probably get you back for it when they hear about it."

"Brothers?" I question, glancing back at her with my brow arched. "Why does it involve all of them when I only insulted one, and only after he insulted me first?"

"That doesn't matter." She glances over her shoulder at her house, then looks back at me. "My brothers are sort of a package deal. Insult one, you insult them all. And some of them take that stuff pretty personally."

"Okay." Why is she warning me? If that's what she's even doing.

She must read the confusion on my face because she sighs. "You're new around this town, aren't you?"

I nod. "We just moved here from Sunnyvale."

"Okay, well, here's a little bit of advice that's going to put you ahead of the game. My brothers are known around Honeyton as troublemakers. And they more than exceed their reputation."

A drop of worry prickles inside me, but I shrug it off. I refuse to be worried about some asshole. I'm tougher than that and have had to deal with guys like him before. Sure, I'm not a fan of doing so, but that doesn't mean I can't handle it.

"Well, just so you know, I'm a retaliating sort of girl,"

I tell her. "Maybe you should warn your brothers about that."

Her lips almost quirk into a smile, but she wrestles it back. "For your sake, I'm not going to. It'll only make things worse." She offers me a partially remorseful look then whirls around and hikes back to her house.

Blowing out a breath, I shove thoughts of the neighbors behind me and duck inside the shed/garage, determined to find a way to get ahold of the landlord.

The space is pretty much empty, so I quickly give up, close it back up, and head back to the car.

"Hey, so, do you want to stay here with Bailey and Payton and keep an eye on our stuff while I go drive around town and try to find Dad's truck?" I ask Londyn.

"Sure." She starts for the porch, but I capture her arm.

"Keep an eye on the neighbors, okay?" I say quietly. "The girl who lives there just gave me some weird warning about how her brothers are going to pay me back for insulting blondie earlier."

Her lips curve downward. "That's a little creepy."

I let go of her arm. "Just make sure to keep an eye out."

She nods then motions for Bailey to follow her.

As Bailey passes me, she pats me on the back. "Glad to see you're still good at making friends, sis."

"Don't you know it," I tease back.

But all my humor dies as I climb into the car and note someone watching me from the upstairs window of the house next door.

Great, only an hour here and I've already stirred up drama.

CHAPTER FOUR

Searching for my dad ends up being a bust.

After driving around for over an hour, I give up and return to the house, convinced he must have left town or something. The area is too small not to be able to find him, and from what I could tell, I looked practically everywhere, except for in the hills.

By the time I pull up into the driveway, it's late and everyone is getting grumpy. I decide to break in through a cracked open window since we can't afford to crash in a hotel.

Once we get all our stuff inside, we dig out some sleeping bags and set them up on the dusty brown carpet in the living room.

"This is by far the worst move ever," Bailey mutters

as she wiggles around in her sleeping bag, trying to get comfortable.

Payton sneezes from all the dust floating around. She has her flashlight app on, giving us a bit of light since the place doesn't have the power turned on yet, even though I called and had it scheduled to turn on. It's too late to get it taken care of now.

"I don't know," she says, rubbing her nose. "Move six was pretty bad."

I fluff my pillow then lie down. "Was that the one where the toilet flooded the basement two days after we moved in?"

"Yep." Payton sneezes again, her eyes watering. "Everything smelled like moldy shit for a month."

"Move five was pretty bad, too," Londyn says as she slips into her sleeping bag that's beside mine.

"Which one was that?" I ask, setting an alarm on my phone so we can get up bright and early and figure out what to do about our situation.

"The one with the rat's nest in the attic." Londyn rolls to her side, facing me. "Honestly, none of them have been that great."

"Yeah, I know." I wiggle around, trying to get situated on the thin carpet.

I did a quick walk-through when we got in and discovered that only half the rooms have carpet, the other half have linoleum flooring. The kitchen is bigger than what we've had before, but it doesn't have a microwave or dishwasher, and there's only one bathroom.

"At least we have a roof over our heads," I attempt optimism.

"One day, I'm afraid we won't," Bailey mumbles, curling up into a ball and pulling the sleeping bag over her head.

"That will never happen," I assure her, reaching over Payton to give her shoulder a squeeze. "I won't let it."

"You won't always be here," Bailey whispers. "You have one more year left of high school, and then you're going to take off to college and we're going to be stuck here with Dad."

Guilt tightens my chest. I want to tell her everything will be okay, but the words won't leave my lips. The truth is, I have no idea what will happen once I pack up my stuff and take off for college. I haven't really thought about it too much, never allowed myself to think about it. But deep down, I know the change is going to affect them big time, and that makes me feel guilty.

"Stop worrying. I can handle things," Londyn assures me, as if reading my mind.

"I'm not worrying," I lie. "Well, not about that."

"Then, what are you worrying about?"

"Where Dad is, the power getting turned on, getting ahold of the landlord."

"So, the usual things."

"Yep."

Silence encases us, except for the soft sound of music floating from somewhere outside.

"Do you think we'll ever stop moving?" Payton wonders. "I mean, while we're living with Dad?"

I want to tell her yes, but I can't bring myself to lie. "I'm not sure."

Sadly, I can't envision our dad suddenly becoming responsible again and taking care of the bills in a timely manner so we won't get evicted. And honestly, in the back of my mind, where my imagination sometimes runs crazy, I wonder if perhaps our dad does it on purpose. That he moves us around so frequently because he's running away from something.

"Night," I whisper to my sisters as Payton turns off her phone. "Love you."

"Love you, too," Londyn mutters sleepily.

"Love all your crazy asses," Bailey mutters through a yawn.

"Love you guys, too." Payton sneezes. "I don't love this fucking dust, though."

"We'll clean it up tomorrow." I roll over to my side.

No one says anything more, and a handful of moments later, Payton starts snoring.

As my eyelids start to grow heavy, I swear I hear a thump from either in the house or just outside.

On edge, I turn on my flashlight app, climb out of the sleeping bag, and do a quick search of the house, but I stumble across nothing and it's too dark outside to see much of anything.

Giving up, I climb back into my sleeping bag, and it ends up taking me half the night before my eyelids lower shut again.

CHAPTER FIVE

"Hadley, wake up." Someone shakes my shoulder.

I wish they'd go away. I'm having the best dream about going off to college. I live in a nice one-bedroom apartment that has a *dishwasher*.

"Hadley, wake up." They shake me again.

Ugh.

No, I don't want to wake up. I want to stay here in my dream ...

But the apartment fades as Bailey appears in front of me, a bruise on her cheek.

"Why did you leave us?" She pouts.

"What happened to your face?" I ask worriedly.

"Dad hit me," she says with tears falling down her cheeks. "He smacked me across the face because I told him off."

"That happened to me once." My cheek begins to burn. "Recently actually."

"I'm sorry, honey." My mom suddenly appears in the dream.

"Mommy." I start to sob as I throw my arms around her.

"Shh ... It's going to be okay." She hugs me tightly.

"No, it's not," I sob. "Everything's broken without you here."

She hugs me tighter. "I know."

"Will you ...? Will you please come back?" I move back to look at her, but she starts to fade away. "Mom!"

She vanishes.

Then I'm suddenly standing near the street with a river flowing on the other side, car engines filling the air. I hear tires skidding, followed by a loud splash.

"No!" my dad shouts from beside me. Then he rushes toward the river, leaving me behind in a mob of bystanders.

I start to run after him, but my stomach clenches as someone screams and I'm—

"Hadley!"

My eyes pop open, and I bolt upright, my cheek throbbing in pain, my skin drenched in sweat. It takes a couple of panicked breaths to get my bearings, to realize I'm not at the scene of my mom's accident. That I'm sitting up in my sleeping bag that's spread across the floor of my new home, sunlight trickling in through the grimy windows. On one side of me is Payton's sleeping bag, and on the other is Londyn's. Bailey is kneeling beside my feet, already dressed in a pair of black jeans and a matching shirt, her hair pulled into a ponytail, and worry written on her face.

"What time is it?" I ask, rubbing my sleepy eyes and trying to rub away the lingering images of the accident.

"Almost ten o'clock." She continues to observe me in concern.

My hands fall to my lap. "Why didn't my alarm go off?"

She wavers. "It did, but we turned it off."

"Why?"

"Well, mostly because we were trying to figure out what to do."

I comb my fingers through my tangled hair. "With Dad?"

"No." Her gaze zeroes in on my cheek. "Your cheek looks really gnarly."

"Don't change the subject." I throw the sleeping bag off me and rise to my feet. "What happened? And where's Payton and Londyn?"

Bailey chews on her bottom lip. "Outside … looking at the damage."

Worry instantly rushes through me. "The damage to what?"

When she doesn't answer, I dash out of the room. I don't bother changing out of my plaid pajama shorts and tank top as I barrel out the door and into the warm August air of Honeyton.

We arrived late enough last night that I didn't get a good look at the neighborhood. Part of me was hoping that perhaps it'd look better in the daylight. If anything, it looks worse. The entire street is covered with dilapidated two-story houses, yellowing front yards, and the occasional junkyard. But we've lived in places equally as bad before.

"Great pick, Dad," I mutter as I jog toward my car where Londyn and Payton are huddled together. "What're you guys doing?"

They jump away from each other, Londyn pressing her hand against her chest and Payton gasping.

"Holy crap, are you part ninja or something?" Payton jokes nervously as she works to catch her breath.

I stop in front of them, my gaze dancing back and forth between them. "Why are you guys acting so twitchy? Bailey said something about something being damaged."

Bailey moves up beside me, and the three of them exchange worried looks. It's unusual for me to be the outsider, but I totally feel like one right now.

I put my hands on my hips. "All right, whatever you did, fess up."

"We didn't do anything." Bailey rubs her hand across

her forehead. "It was just like that when we came out here."

"What was like what?" I track her gaze to my car, and my worry skyrockets. "What happened to my car?"

Londyn frowns, while Payton looks away, and Bailey chews on her fingernail.

Giving up, I circle the car to see if I can find out for myself …

"What the fuck?" My lips part in shock as I spot one, two, three, *four* … "How the hell are all my tires flat?"

"It gets worse," Payton mumbles, scuffing the tip of her shoe against the dirt.

I look to Londyn for help.

Sighing, she rounds to the trunk and pops it open. "There're some, um, car pieces from the engine, I think, in here. I'm not sure which ones since I don't know shit about cars."

Anger simmers under my skin as I march to the back of the car to look inside the trunk. Sure enough, pieces of the carburetor, along with the battery are scattered around inside.

Fuming, I stride around to the front of the car and pop the hood. I'm not even sure why I bother looking. The parts are for sure mine. Just as I'm pretty sure I know who did this.

"Car trouble?" The sound of blondie baby douchebag's mocking tone makes my lips curl.

I reel around, preparing to have a throw down with him, but instantly falter.

Standing on the other side of the fence beside blondie are two guys, one who looks barely a bit younger with chin-length black hair and the bluest eyes I've ever seen, and the other looks slightly older with dark hair, a few facial piercings, heavily inked arms., and dark circles under his eyes All of them share similar facial features, so I'm guessing they're brothers. They're also dressed head to toe in black with a different assortment of studded bracelets, belts, and chains decorating their outfits, as if they're auditioning for a Goth boy band. A very pretty Goth boy band.

Why is it the douchey ones are always pretty?

A smirk starts to rise on blondie baby douchebag's face, and I realize I'm staring at them.

Pulling my head out of my ass, I glare at him. "Did you fucking do this to my car?"

"Someone did something to your car?" He feigns dumb yet keeps on smirking. "Wow, that really sucks."

I narrow my eyes at him. "Don't pretend like you didn't do it. I know you did."

He stares me down hard. "If you're so sure, then prove it."

I want to pick up a rock and throw it at his stupid pretty face, but the last thing my family needs right now is assault charges pressed against me.

Blondie rests his arms on top of the fence. "You know, my brother over here"—he nods at the older-looking one—"is a mechanic. And maybe, if you ask really, really nicely, he might just fix your car for you."

My narrowed gaze snaps to the alleged mechanic of the three, and he smirks.

"I don't know, Blaise." He flashes blondie a conniving grin. "I'm not sure she's pretty enough to entice me to do much of anything."

My hands ball into fists. Screw this. I need to punch something, mess up Goth bands' pretty boy faces.

Suddenly, Londyn strides forward and snags the back of my shirt, towing me back—I didn't even realize I was stepping forward. Then she positions herself in front of me protectively.

"Who the hell do you guys think you are?" she spits furiously. "Don't you ever talk to my sister that way. And stay the hell away from her damn car!"

As much as I appreciate her protectiveness, her bodyguard act is probably going to escalate the situation.

I step to the side of her and mumble under my breath, "I'm not sure this is the best way to handle the situation."

She turns to me, her eyes wild with anger. "We can't just let them get away with this. They slashed the tires and broke ... well, whatever the hell that was in the trunk. And they practically called you ugly, which you so aren't." She raises her voice and glowers at them. "And they know it. They're just being bullies because you shot dickhead over there down." She waves her hand in Blaise's direction.

As their sister's warning flicks through my thoughts, I grab Londyn's arm and draw her behind me.

Yes, I'm pissed off at the next-door neighbors, and in no way in hell do I plan on letting this go, but I need to keep my sisters out of this. Let the asshats focus on me.

I catch Londyn's gaze. "I need you to do me a favor. Take Payton and Bailey inside so I can handle this."

She promptly shakes her head. "There's no way I'm leaving you out here to deal with those three." She blasts a glare at the guys.

They grin in response.

"I'm not going to deal with them." *Lie.* I'm totally going to fight back, because I have a feeling they might see it as a weakness if I don't. And I can sense these guys thrive off weakness. "I just need to get the car put back together so we can go get the utilities turned on, track down the landlord, and go look for Dad."

She wiggles her arm free from my grip. "Then, why do we have to go inside?"

I shrug. "Because I can't concentrate with you out here."

She crosses her arms, her brow rising in challenge. "I'm not going anywhere."

I internally sigh, racking my brain for a better way to get rid of her. "Actually, you know what? Instead of going into the house, can you walk to the gas station a few blocks down and buy a can of Fix-A-Flat?"

Yeah, there's no way a can of Fix-A-Flat is going to help my completely flat tires, but Londyn is clueless when it comes to cars, so she'll more than likely buy in to my bullshit. Then, once she's gone, I can figure out how to handle this situation. Rationally, hopefully, but more than likely doubtful.

No, messing with my car was their way of declaring neighborly war on my ass and trying to show me who rules around here. But they can go fuck themselves if they think I'm going to back down.

"Fine," Londyn finally agrees. "But I'm leaving Bailey here."

My lips part to protest, but she's already walking away.

"That's not up for argument."

"Yes, Mom," I call out, shaking my head.

When did she become so bossy? And toward me? I can't even recall the last time I was bossed around.

Once Payton and her start down the road, I turn to Bailey.

She lifts a brow. "So, what're you going to do?"

"I'm not sure yet." I give a sidelong glance at the three guys who have now pulled out some fold-up chairs and taken a seat by the fence.

The oldest of the three kicks his boots up on top of the fence and leans back in the chair with his arms tucked behind his head, his eyes on me, a smirk playing at his lips. The black-haired one doesn't appear quite as amused as he props his foot up on his knee and pops open a can of beer.

"Don't mind us. We're just here to watch the show," the oldest one calls out, grinning.

"Please continue, *sweetheart*." Blaise grins. "We're getting bored."

"Sweetheart?" The oldest cocks his head to the side, surveying me. "She doesn't seem like the sweetheart type."

"Yeah, but she's not a baby sort of girl either." Blaise is all smirks and wickedness, yet underneath the amusement, he seems a bit irritated. Why, I haven't got a damn clue nor a care.

"Still, you can't call her sweetheart," the other replies musingly. "It doesn't fit."

Blaise's smile is all wickedness. "Then, what should we call her?"

The older one rubs his jawline. "How about princess?"

Blaise shakes his head. "Nah, that doesn't fit her either."

"What's her name?" the one who's barely spoken asks Blaise.

"I have no idea." Blaise looks at me expectantly.

I flip him the middle finger. "Go fuck yourself."

Blaise chuckles. "We really need to start working on your nicknames for me, sweetheart." He slants forward, resting his hands on his knees. "I get it. You're shy and probably a little flustered. That's understandable." He winks. "We have that effect on people."

When I give him a blank stare, his smile enlarges.

"All right, since I can tell you're still a little reluctant, I'll go first." He presses his hand to his chest. "I'm Blaise. And this is my brother, Jaxon," He gestures at the black-haired one with the crazy blue eyes.

Jaxon does nothing but keep his gaze fixed on me as he takes a swig of beer.

"He's a man of few words," Blaise explains, then motions at the oldest of the three, the one with all the tattoos and piercings. "And this is my other brother, Alex."

"But since I'm the mechanic and the one you're going to have to convince to fix your car, you should probably come up with a better name to call me, like maybe sexy beast or master—something along those lines." Alex smirks amusedly. "Although, I think we already decided she isn't enticing enough for me."

I've grown quiet, stunned. Sure, I've had to deal with jerks before, but these three are beyond the realms of normal asshatery. In fact, they're so asshole-ish, I think they need their very own dickhead term. Like dick-prick-dumb-fuckers-stupid-fucking-asshole-shits!

I'm about to declare their nickname to the entire neighborhood when Bailey steps up beside me.

"We need to shut them the hell up," she growls with her hands balled into fists.

She's ready for a fight, and so am I, but not a physical one. No, as tough as I can be, I'm not stupid enough to believe Bailey and I can take these guys on. Plus, I don't want her fighting.

I crack my knuckles against the sides of my legs. "Go get my toolbox. It's in the living room beside my box of clothes."

"Why?"

"Just do it."

Grimacing, she strides off toward the front door of the house. Neither of the guys even glance at her, too fixated on trying to make me squirm under their mocking gazes.

Lifting my chin, I square my shoulders and march to my trunk. After securing my hair in a messy bun, I pull out a folded-up blanket, spread it out on the ground, and begin taking the carburetor's pieces out.

"What's she doing?" Alex asks, his tone laced with confusion, yet his eyes sparkle with mischief.

"I'm not sure." Blaise eyes me over with a crinkle at his brows. "But she's definitely trying to do something."

"I think she's going to try to put it back together," Jaxon remarks, then takes another swig of beer.

While I'm betting he's about my age and is drinking illegally, I'm not that surprised he's doing it out in the open. Sadly, most everyone around here more than likely doesn't care. It's been the same way in a lot of neighborhoods we've lived in.

Once I get the pieces all set up, Bailey has returned with my tools. She doesn't question what I'm doing, only grins as she puts two and two together.

Kneeling on the blanket, I pull out a set of screwdrivers, wrenches, and pliers. Then I get to work, moving as quickly as I can, but not so fast that I mess up. As the sun starts to rise higher over the hills, sweat begins to bead on my skin. Well, at least I try to blame the sweating on the heat. Really, it may have something to do with having an audience. A very freakin' annoying audience.

They watch me the entire time I work, whispering amongst each other and occasionally talking loud enough for me to hear their insults. Doesn't really matter. In the end, I have the final say after I get the carburetor put back together, attach it to the engine, and then reinstall the battery. Then, just for an added emphasis on how badass I am, I slide into the driver's seat and twist the key. The engine grumbles to life, just like I knew it would—I never second-guess my work when it comes to cars.

Wiping my greasy hands on the side of my shorts, I turn the car off, hop out, and Bailey and I fist bump. Then I turn to the guys, cross my arms, and smile sweetly.

"Thanks for taking that apart for me. I've been meaning to see if I can break my record time of putting it back together."

Blaise and Alex trade an indecipherable look, then Blaise faces me, his lips parting.

I hold up my hand. "Nope, *sweetheart*, you had your turn. Now it's mine." I step toward him. "I don't know what sort of people you're used to dealing with, but I'm not going to let you walk all over me or my sisters, so back the hell off, or you're going to regret it."

Blaise rises from his chair. "Is that a threat?"

"Yep. And here it is again, because you seem a little slow." I step closer to the fence, so close I can see the muscles in Blaise's jaw pulsating. "Stay away from me and my sisters, or you're going to regret it."

He folds his lean arms across his chest and slips his

tongue out to wet his lips, the glint of a metal piercing reflecting in the sunlight, his dark gaze boring into me.

"You okay?" Jaxon asks Blaise, his brows crinkled, appearing confused for who the hell knows what reason.

"Yep," Blaise says while staring at me.

Holding my gaze for a slamming heartbeat longer, he then tears his eyes off me and strides toward the house.

"See you around, Hadley," he calls over his shoulder.

What the hell? How did he learn my name? And why did he pretend earlier that he didn't know it? Maybe he heard one of my sisters say it.

Great. I don't want him knowing my name. I don't want him knowing anything about me or my sisters.

Alex jogs after Blaise, catching up with him on the front porch. With a heavy sigh, Jaxon pushes to his feet and walks away, too.

Once they're gone, I twist around to face Bailey. "Well, that was intense."

"Super intense." She looks over at their house then back at me. "Dude, I have a bad feeling about those guys. Like, they're going to try to get you back for threatening them."

I know that, and I'm worried I might have just poked a sleeping badger. Not wanting to freak her out, though, I put on my fake smile. "Everything's going to be fine. I'm sure they're all bark and no bite."

She gives a pressing glance at my car. "Yeah, that's why you have four flat tires and just spent the last half hour putting your car back together."

I dismiss her with a wave of my hand. "It's just a car. No biggie."

No biggie, Hadley. It's our only source of transportation at the moment.

But I keep my calm face on, faking it like I often do.

"No biggie?" Bailey shakes her head incredulously. "We currently have no place to live, no power, no food, and now we don't have a vehicle. We're seriously fucked up the ass."

"Hey, watch your mouth," I scold, but she only rolls her eyes. Sighing, I circle my car to examine the tires again. "I wonder if they slashed them or just let the air out."

"Did you see the evil smirks on their face?" Bailey questions. "They definitely slashed them."

A sigh slips from my lips. "Yeah, I know."

Bailey kicks one of the tires with the tip of her boot. "How are we going to get them fixed? We can't afford it."

"Yeah, I know." Those seem to be my go-to words at the moment.

Usually, I'm better at hiding my worry from my

sisters, but those guys have me frazzled.

I need to get my shit together.

"Here, give me your phone." I stick out my hand.

"Why?"

"Because I'm going to get a quote on some tires, then I'm going to call Dad."

"He's not going to pick up." She hands me her phone. "Londyn already tried, like, five times this morning."

"Well, I'm going to try again." I open her internet app and search local tire stores.

"Why? It's pointless." She plops down on the blanket I used while putting together the carburetor. "Even if he does answer his phone, he's not going to help us."

"He can give me the name of the landlord and their phone number."

"And then what? Because my bet is he hasn't even paid the deposit yet." She stretches her legs out. "Honestly, at this point, I'm starting to wonder if perhaps he ever even rented this place. I think he told us some bullshit story so he could ditch us out in the middle of some redneck town."

The thought has crossed my mind that perhaps our dad really has been running away from something for the last eight years and has finally decided to do it solo.

"I'm sure that's not what—"

A car suddenly zooms down the road and peels into

the driveway next door, kicking up a cloud of dirt.

"Holy hell, it's your long-lost twin." Bailey coughs, fanning her hand in front of her face as dust funnels around us.

I eyeball the car, a 1969 GTO Judge, black with red racing stripes. "Pretty."

Bailey points at me. "Don't get mesmerized yet. It could be one of *their* cars." She glares at the house the car is parked in front of. I assume she is referring to Blaise, Alex, and Jaxon.

"No way. They just went inside." I openly check the car out, my chest filling with envy.

What I wouldn't give to have my car looking that fantastic. And with functional tires.

Bailey and I watch as the driver's door swings open and a guy hops out. Tall, with short, dark brown hair, he looks around my age, and almost as attractive as Blaise. He's dressed in similar attire as Blaise, Jaxon, and Alex were—all black with chains dangling off his belt loops, thick boots covering his feet, and leather bands decorating his wrists.

"Yummy," Bailey mutters, biting her bottom lip.

"No yummy," I warn. "I'm pretty sure he's related to dipshit one, two, and three."

"How can you tell?"

"Because he looks like them."

She pouts. "Well, that sucks."

"Why? Were you planning on going over there and hitting on him?" I tease as I stare at my car.

"No." Her lie shines through her tone and how she turns her head away to hide her smile.

"You're such a little liar." Flashing her a teasing grin, I move to dial a nearby tire company's phone number. "Besides, I thought hitting on guys was more Payton's thing—"

"Is that your ride?" a deep, male voice sails from over my shoulder.

I trade a wary look with Bailey before turning around. Sure enough, Mr. Yummy himself is standing beside the fence with a soft smile dancing at his lips. Although, unlike Blaise, Alex, and Jaxon, his smile doesn't look malicious.

"Yeah," I reply cautiously.

"It's not too bad. Would look even better if it was fixed up." He dazzles me with a grin, but his brows furrow as his gaze sweeps over me.

What? Has he never seen a girl in greasy pajamas before?

"It looks fine as is," I reply flatly.

"I didn't mean anything by it," he quickly adds. "I was just trying to give you a compliment."

"Well, thanks, I guess." I begin to turn back around, but apparently, he's not done with the conversation yet.

"I'd like to see how it races sometime," he continues.

"There's a place down by the river where some people get together. You should come down there sometime. I think there might be a race going on this weekend."

Bailey leans in toward me and whispers, "I'm pretty sure the hottest guy I've ever seen is hitting on you right now."

"He's not hitting on me. In fact, I'm pretty sure he's up to something." Facing him again, I recline against my car. "Thanks for the invite, but until I can come up with the cash to get four new tires, I won't be taking this out racing anytime soon."

His brows knit. "How did all of your tires go flat?"

I point at the house behind him. "Dipshit one, dipshit two, and dipshit three decided to welcome me to the neighborhood."

His jaw tightens. "You've met my brothers?"

So, he is related to the asshats next door. Dammit, I was hoping he wasn't.

"Yep." I move to leave. "It was nice meeting you …" I realize I don't know his name.

Gripping the top of the fence, he easily hoists himself over it. Then he walks toward me with his hand outstretched. "I'm Rhyland, and I really want to apologize for whatever my brothers did or said to you."

Still wary of him, I don't shake his hand. "It's fine. You didn't do it."

"Yeah, but they're my brothers." He sighs loudly.

"And we're supposed to watch out for each other and make sure we don't do anything stupid. But I've been distracted lately and haven't been doing a very good job."

I feel a bit of empathy for him. "I get that. I really do. I have three younger sisters and my dad ..." I clear my throat. The last thing I need is to tell a stranger about my dad. "Anyway, it's sort of my job to keep an eye on them and make sure they stay out of trouble. I fail, though, a lot."

He watches me with interest. "I doubt that. I'm sure you're just being too hard on yourself."

"Tell that to the countless times I've had to pick one of them up from jail or bail them out of a bad situation." I shake my head. I can't be telling him this sort of stuff, not with Blaise being his brother. "But anyway, it was nice meeting you ..." Shit, I forgot his name.

Fuck, I need to start getting better sleep.

A smile graces his lips. "Rhyland."

"Right, Rhyland." I roll my eyes at myself. "It was really nice meeting you, Rhyland."

"It was *really* nice meeting you, too." He catches my gaze. "I'd really like to know your name, though."

I almost don't want to give it to him, but I figure he'll probably learn it soon anyway. "It's Hadley."

"It's nice to meet you, Hadley." He smiles while offering me his hand to shake again.

Instead of shaking it, I tap my knuckles against his, because hand shaking is weird.

He chuckles, but then he frowns when his gaze lands on my car. "Let me buy some new tires for you. It's the least I can do to make up for what my brothers did."

What I wouldn't give to be able to accept that offer, but my pride gets the best of me.

"No, thank you. I can take care of it."

"Please," he practically begs. "I really want to."

I'm about to decline again when my dad's truck pulls into the driveway.

"Oh, look, he finally found his way here," Bailey mumbles with irritation.

I turn toward Rhyland, preparing to say goodbye so I can take care of the endless list of stuff I need to do, but he's already over the fence and heading toward his house.

So much for being friendly.

My guard goes up as I watch him walk away, wondering if his nice guy, gentleman act might have been just that—an act.

"All right, who's ready to see the new house?" my dad announces as he gets out of the truck.

He's cleaned up a bit since I last saw him. Or, well, at least changed his clothes, which is considered cleaned up for him.

"Where the hell have you been?" I demand as I stride toward him.

Between having to break in last night to waking up to dealing with our new neighbors, I'm feeling a bit testy. And his blasé attitude about ditching us last night is only adding fuel to the wildfire.

"Picking up the keys for our new place, getting the power and water turned on, and finding a job." He pats my shoulder. "Thanks for taking care of things last night."

I grind my jaw from side to side. "I had to break in to a house I wasn't even sure was ours, just so we didn't have to sleep in the car. Where were you all night? Because I know you weren't getting the keys for this place and finding a new job at two o'clock in the morning."

He scrubs his hand over his head. "I was taking care of some other stuff."

"You mean, finding out which bar lets you open a tab?" I question. "Or which bar has the most inattentive bartender so you can hand him a fake credit card, then stiff the bill altogether?"

"That's not what I do." But his guilt is written all over his face.

"I know your scams, Dad." I back away, shaking my head. "In case you've forgotten, I'm the one who's had to go down to the bar and pay your outstanding tabs, or convince the bar owner that you just forgot to pay the bill and weren't trying to take off."

"I wasn't scamming anyone over last night," he bites out. "I really did have some stuff to take care of."

I don't believe him. I'd be stupid to.

"So, where's your new job then?"

He shrugs, scuffing the tip of his boot against the dirt. "Around here."

"Mmhmm." I roll my eyes. Sure it is. "And what exactly are you going to be doing?"

"Stuff." He tosses me a set of keys before hiking to the back of his truck. "It requires me to be gone a lot. I might even be gone for a week at a time, so I'm counting on you to take care of your sisters."

"I always do," I mutter.

God knows what the hell he's actually doing for work. Probably something illegal. Or he might even be lying about having a job altogether. Wouldn't be the first time.

The last time he pulled a stunt like that, he pretended to go to work every morning, only to spend the entire day at the bar, spending what little money we had on whiskey. It took me three weeks to catch on after I realized no money was coming in. I ended up tailing him and, sure enough, discovered his dirty little secret.

After that, I started keeping an eye on him. That was

also when I got my first part-time job. I was fourteen and lied about my age to get a waitressing job at a café. I've been working part-time jobs ever since. So do my sisters. It's how we buy food, school clothes, and other necessities, and pay the bills when needed. It's never enough, though, hence the constant moving. It doesn't help that our dad is always either borrowing money from us or stealing it when we refuse to give him any cash.

After Dad drops the tailgate, Bailey and I start helping him move stuff inside the house. Eventually, Londyn and Payton return with a can of Fix-A-Flat.

"What happened to your tires?" Dad asks as he follows me with a box in his hands.

"The neighbors," I answer as I set the can of Fix-A-Flat on the hood of my car.

He blinks in confusion. "They flattened your tires? Why?"

"We got off on the wrong foot, I guess."

"Do you want me to go talk to them?"

I quickly shake my head. "No, I can handle it."

Adjusting the box underneath his arm, he scratches his head. "I think maybe we should keep our distance from the people around here." When I give him a puzzled look, he adds, "I just don't think we're going to be here very long, and I don't want you girls getting attached to anyone."

"We never do." A bit of annoyance rings in my tone.

He doesn't seem to notice, giving me a pat on my shoulder before walking into the house.

I start to turn back toward the truck to grab some more boxes when my gaze magnetizes toward the neighbors'. Blaise is standing on the front porch and leaning against the railing. His face is mostly shadowed, so I can't see it very well, but I can feel his stare burning into me. And I stare right back. He doesn't look away, and neither do I.

The air starts to burn, scorching hot, as I refuse to let this asshole intimidate me.

"Hadley."

I flinch as Bailey nudges my foot with hers.

"Huh?" I blink at her.

"I asked which room you wanted?" She frowns, her eyes traveling to the neighbors' house. "What were you staring at?"

I dare a glimpse back at Blaise, only to find him gone. "Nothing." I shake my head, trying to clear the unsettling feeling that I somehow just lost a silent battle with Blaise by looking away.

I shouldn't be worried, though. They're just guys. Nothing more.

And I've handled worse.

CHAPTER SIX

My sisters and I spend the rest of the night unloading boxes and furniture into the house. Then we make a quick trip to the grocery store to buy some food. Our dad helps for a bit, but eventually goes up to his room and passes out, most likely hungover.

The house has three bedrooms, so Londyn and I bunk up in one and Payton and Bailey in the other. We don't have much for furniture, just some mattresses, bedframes, and a couple of dressers, so organizing doesn't take too long.

Once we're finished for the night, Londyn climbs into bed, while I stare out the window at the next-door neighbors', playing guard basically. The lights in the house are off, but the back porch light is on, highlighting all the cars in the backyard.

"So, what do you think about Dad already having a job, yet not telling us where he's working?" Londyn asks, fluffing her pillow.

"I'm not sure." I sit down on the dresser and continue to stare out the window. "He could've been lying, or he could be doing something illegal."

"Where do you think he was last night?"

"Probably a bar."

"All night?"

"Wouldn't be the first time."

"Yeah, but … didn't he seem sort of, I don't know, evasive about everything?"

"Isn't that Dad's middle name?" I remind her. "I feel as if I barely know him anymore."

"Me, too," she mumbles through a yawn. "One day, maybe we'll have to do some detective work and figure out what he really does."

"Wouldn't that be funny?" I muse. "To use the detective skills he taught us when we were younger to bust his ass for doing something illegal?"

"It would be pretty funny. He'd probably get pissed off." A beat of silence drags by. "Had, if he ever hits one of us again, I think we should report it to the police."

My fingers drift to my cheek. "I thought about doing that, but at the same time, if the police intervene and Social Services gets called, we might be separated."

My hand falls to my lap. "But if he hits any one of you, I'll do it."

"I wish we could just gain guardianship of each other." Londyn yawns again. "You're almost eighteen and way more responsible than Dad."

"I wish I could, but I'm not sure I can." No, unfortunately, if our dad ever does lose guardianship, my sisters will probably end up in group homes, even though I'll be a legal adult in just a couple weeks.

I remain sitting on the dresser for a few more minutes, staring at the neighbors' backyard, listening to Londyn breathe heavily as she dozes off. Eventually, my eyelids grow heavy and I move to my bed, deciding playing guard all night isn't possible. But the moment I hop off the dresser, a large SUV pulls into their driveway and parks near the porch. The headlights click off, and four figures hop out.

Clicking off the lamp, I hunker down as the figures move toward the house. When they step onto the porch, the porch light casts across their faces, revealing the four figures are none other than Blaise, Alex, Jaxon, and Rhyland.

They appear to be having a heated argument. Blaise is in Alex's face, his hands balled at his sides as he reams into him. Alex stands stiffly with his arms crossed, his lips never parting, while Rhyland and Jaxon watch.

As Blaise continues to bite Alex's head off, his gaze

suddenly darts to my bedroom window. Panicking, I crouch down lower, though there's no way he could have seen me.

With Alex's gaze fixes on my window, he nods once. Then Blaise nods, visibly relaxing and giving Alex's shoulder a pat. He says a few more words, and then the four of them head into the house.

My stomach twists with uneasiness as I tiptoe to my bed, climb in, and spend half the night lying in bed, worrying, before finally falling asleep.

CHAPTER SEVEN

I wake up the next morning feeling as though I spent all night throwing back shots.

I really need to work on getting better sleep.

Combing my fingers through my hair, I shove the blankets off as I look around the mostly bare room. Londyn's bed has already been made and her boxes are emptied out. She must have gotten up really early in order to finish unpacking. Or I just got up late, I realize as I check the time on my phone.

It's almost noon. I never sleep this late, unless I'm hungover.

Frustrated with my laziness, I drag my ass out of bed and tear open the box where all my clothes are stuffed. I dig out a black T-shirt, a pair of jeans, and turn to take a shower, when the house next door snags my attention.

I spent half the night stressed out over if they'd do something else to me. And now I'm exhausted because of it.

I need to stop stressing about stuff so much.

Forcing myself to stop thinking about the neighbors for now, I go to the bathroom to take a quick shower. Then I get dressed and secure my hair into a high ponytail before heading downstairs to get some lunch, since it's already past noon.

When I enter the kitchen, my dad is at the counter, dressed in a jacket, jeans, and work boots, and he's stuffing a sandwich into a baggie.

"Where are you going?" I wonder as I collect a cup from a box and grab the juice from the fridge.

"To work." He tosses the bagged sandwich into a lunchbox and adds a water bottle.

"It's Saturday." I take a sip of my juice.

"Yeah, so? People sometimes have to work on Saturdays." He zips up the lunchbox and collects his new truck key he had made yesterday from the local locksmith. "The job I got actually requires me to work seven days a week."

I nearly drop my cup. "So, you're going to be working every day?"

He nods, crossing the kitchen toward the door. "It's

called a full-time job, Hadley." He exits the house, slamming the door behind him.

I hurry across the kitchen and open the door, stepping out onto the small porch. He's already in his truck and backing down the driveway. He turns right on the road, heading in the opposite direction of the main part of town. I make a mental note of that, wishing my car was functional so I could tail him and find out where he's working.

"How far of a drive is it?"

Voices float from next door as Rhyland, Blaise, Alex, and Jaxon file out of their house and down the front porch. Like yesterday, they're dressed all in black, some with studded belts, some with chains on their beltloop. Rhyland even has studded suspenders hanging from the waistband of his jeans.

"I'm not sure." Alex tosses the keys to Rhyland.

Jaxon sighs tiredly as he reaches a black SUV with tinted windows parked out front. "I don't feel like going to a party today."

Rhyland rounds the front of the car and opens the driver's side door. "It'll be fun. And it's by the lake. You like going to the lake."

"I hate going to the fucking lake," Alex grumbles. "Can I stay home?"

"Nope," Blaise says in a cold tone as he grabs the door handle. "You're already in deep shit over that little stunt you pulled with …" His eyes stray toward my house, quickly finding me. He fleetingly stiffens.

Alex tracks his gaze, his lips tugging up into a smirk. "Gentlemen, we have an audience."

Four sets of eyes lock on me. But that four hastily turns to three as Jaxon yanks open the door and climbs inside the SUV so swiftly you'd think looking at me burned his retinas or something.

"Hey, Hadley," Rhyland greets me with a smile.

"Rhyland," I reply in a formal tone.

He smiles amusedly while dragging his hand across his mouth.

"Where's my greeting?" Blaise questions, partially amused, partially irritated, and if I didn't know any better, a tiny bit hurt.

"Right here." I flip him off.

Alex snorts a laugh as he pulls open the back door to the SUV. "She's so feisty."

"Yeah, I know." Blaise's intense gaze sears into me as he nibbles on his bottom lip. "Maybe I should tame it out of her."

Alex gives him a funny, sort of surprised look.

"Maybe I should tame the asshole out of you," I quip back, flipping Blaise off again.

Blaise's gaze is full of fire as he starts to step toward my house. "I think it might be time you and I—"

"Blaise," Rhyland cuts him off. "What're you doing? You need to calm down. This isn't like you."

Yeah, that statement seems like the biggest lie ever.

Blaise quickly slams to a halt. "Fine, let's just go." He throws one final glance at me, seeming a bit unsettled, then gets in the car.

Rhyland offers me an apologetic look, then jumps into the driver's seat and peels out of the driveway, leaving a cloud of dust behind.

Shaking my head, I step back into the house right as Londyn wanders into the kitchen. She's wearing a pair of soccer shorts, a tank, knee-high socks, shin guards, cleats, a soccer ball is tucked under her arm, and her hair is pulled into a messy bun.

"What were you just doing?" she wonders suspiciously when she notes how close to the door I am. "And please don't tell me you were having a throw down with those jerks next door."

"Okay, I wasn't having a throw down with the jerks next door." I say it more as a question, though.

A weighted sigh puffs from her lips as she opens the fridge. "I was thinking about this all last night. While those guys are infuriating, I think we should keep our distance from them." She grabs a water bottle then bumps the fridge door shut. "You should've heard what the clerk at the gas station was saying about them yesterday when I told him where we lived." She shakes her head, unscrewing the lid off the water bottle. "Apparently, they cause trouble all the time and do some pretty dangerous stuff, but they never get in trouble for it because almost everyone in town is scared of them."

"Almost everyone in town is scared of a bunch of teenage guys?" I question as I pick up a box of granola bars.

She takes a swig of water. "Well, not so much of them, but their dad."

"Who's their dad?"

"I'm not sure. I just heard that he's pretty sketchy."

So weird.

I rest my arms on top of the counter. "Why were you talking to this cashier guy about them?"

She shrugs. "He asked me if I was new here, and when I told him I was and where I lived, he started warning me about our new neighbors. He also offered to help us out if we needed help moving in."

"Hmmm … Sounds like he was hitting on you."

"No, it wasn't like that." But a wistful smile tugs at her lips. "It wouldn't be so terrible if he was, though. He was pretty hot and seemed sweet." Screwing the cap back on the water bottle, she starts for the door. "I'm going to hit up the park and do some practice drills. Text me if you need anything." She waves goodbye before slipping out of the house, leaving me to wonder if the cashier guy's warning has any truth to it.

Could the neighbors be dangerous?

One thing is for sure. I need to make sure they stay away from my sisters.

CHAPTER EIGHT

THE NEXT WEEK PASSES BY SWIFTLY AND SURPRISINGLY without any more drama. We get settled into the house, I celebrate my eighteenth birthday with my sisters, just hanging out and relaxing, something I greatly appreciate. Londyn and I find a part-time job delivering newspapers in the mornings, and Bailey and Payton get hired to babysit the neighbors' kids after school. Not the neighbors' right next door to us. No, I haven't seen or heard much from them, which is a relief.

School starts today, and I have a feeling I'm going to be bumping into them in the hallways.

Once my alarm goes off, I get up, take a shower, then pull on my favorite pair of black jeans, a black tank top, and top the look off with a plaid overshirt, a velvet choker, and a pair of thick boots. I leave my hair down in wild waves swept to the side, and then I trace my eyes with kohl eyeliner.

Usually, I'm a bit more nervous about starting a new school, but since it's the beginning of a new school year, it's not quite as stressful. Plus, it's the start of my senior year. The start of my very last year of high school. Then I get to go off to college.

I fist-pump the air before turning to walk out of my room, running into Londyn in the hallway. I follow her downstairs where Bailey and Payton are munching on granola bars and waiting for us.

I hurriedly grab a couple of granola bars for myself then usher everyone out the door, knowing we have a long walk ahead of us.

"Do we really have to walk?" Bailey gripes as I lock the door.

I nod, stuffing the keys into my pocket. "Sorry, but until we can come up with some cash for new tires, we're going to be trekking around on foot for a—what the hell!" I sputter as I catch sight of my car.

Bailey's brows furrow then a smile spreads across her face as she tracks my gaze. "Your tires are fixed!" She does a little happy dance. "Hell yeah! No walking to school."

I look at Londyn. "Did you do this?"

She shakes her head. "I wish I did, but I'm as broke as you are."

I give Payton a suspicious glance. "Did you by chance find a way to steal four new tires?"

"No, but I did think about it." She drums her finger against her lips. "Maybe Dad did it?"

Silence stretches between us, then we bust up laughing.

"Yeah, right." I wipe the tears of laughter from my eyes. "And then, after that, he prepaid all our bills, so we never have to worry about getting evicted again."

"God, wouldn't that be nice?" Londyn says as we open the doors to get into my car.

"Definitely …" I pause, noticing a small card balanced on the dashboard.

I grab the card and open it.

Hadley,

Sorry about what my brother did to your tires. I know this doesn't make up for him, but I'm hoping it's a start.

From,

Your neighbor

I rub the back of my hand across my forehead as I slowly drop into the driver's seat.

"Who's that from?" Londyn asks as she shuts the door.

I hand her the note then slip the keys into the ignition and start up the engine.

She reads over the note, and then a silly grin touches her lips. "Well, that was sort of nice, I guess. But which one of them do you think did it?"

"My guess is Rhyland. He seems the nicest. Definitely not Blaise." I clutch the steering wheel, unsure what to make of the card. "I don't know about this … I mean, I'm glad we have tires now, but I feel like maybe there's more to it than him just putting new tires on my car."

Londyn sets the card down on the console then reaches to put her seatbelt on. "You think he has an ulterior motive?"

I shift the car into reverse. "Maybe."

Londyn nods. "After what Hunter told me, I wouldn't trust any of them."

"Who's Hunter?" Bailey, Payton, and I ask simultaneously.

"The cashier at the gas station." Her cheeks redden a bit.

Jeez, has she already fallen for this guy?

"Are you dating him or something?" Because she has been "practicing soccer drills" a lot lately.

"No," she scoffs, but her blush deepens.

I trade an amused grin with Payton and Bailey, but my grin erases as my gaze lands on the card.

Bailey tracks my gaze then leans over the seat. "You think they fixed your tires as a prank or something?"

"What kind of a prank is that?" Payton points out as she draws her seatbelt over her shoulder.

"I'm not sure." I start to press on the gas, but then hesitate. Pushing the shifter back into park, I fasten my seatbelt. "Put your seatbelt on, Bailey."

She eyeballs me warily before sitting back and doing what she's told.

"What exactly do you think's going to happen?" Londyn asks with mild concern.

"I don't know." I really don't either. All I know is that, according to the note, my neighbor put new tires on my car sometime last night while I was asleep—I would've noticed if it was before last night. But maybe Blaise had Alex, the mechanic of the brothers, put on the tires to distract me from something else they did to my car. Something bad.

I do a quick brake check before backing out onto the street. Then I hold my breath as I drive forward. I continue to hold my breath for a few blocks. The farther we get without any mishaps, the more I question if maybe I'm being paranoid.

That theory seems more plausible when we arrive at school without any mishaps and quite a bit early, since we were originally planning on walking.

When I turn off the engine, a breath of relief escapes my lips.

"Well," Payton says, "guess you were wrong about

Mr. Fine Ass next door, which means I can ask him out, right?"

I swiftly shake my head. "No dating any of them, understand? They're way too old for you, and from what Londyn's told me, they could be dangerous."

"They are so not too old for me," Payton argues. "Jaxon, the youngest, is a little bit older than Londyn. And Blaise is just a bit older than you." She points at me then pulls a tube of lip gloss from her pocket. "And Alex and Rhyland are just a couple months younger than Blaise. Rhyland and Alex are twins and half-brothers to Blaise and Jaxon, who are not even a year apart in age."

"And we thought our parents had us close," I mutter to myself.

"Yeah, I know," she agrees with a nod. "They all have the same dad and everything, but he's a big-time player from what people say and considering they're all close in age, but Jaxon and Blaise have a different mom as Alex and Rhyland, I can see why people think that."

I rotate around in the seat and gape at her. "How in the hell did you get all that information?"

She applies a coat of lip gloss and shrugs. "Miss Clammersin—the lady we're babysitting for—likes to gossip, so I asked her about the Porterson brothers, you know, in case we need some intel on them. And she was more than happy to oblige."

I lift a brow. "The Porterson brothers?"

"That's what people around here call them." She stuffs her lip gloss back into her pocket. "Rhyland and Alex are twins and, from what Miss Clammersin said, Blaise is pretty much like the parent of the household. I'm not sure why. But she did say they have quite the reputation for causing trouble. Even worse than us, probably."

"Blaise is like the parent of the household?" I question, stunned. "Well, doesn't that just sound lovely?"

"You're basically like the parent to us," Payton reminds me as she checks her phone.

"But I don't go around slitting people's tires because they didn't swoon at my feet when I called them baby," I point out, tucking the keys into my pocket.

Payton's brow curves up. "What about the time you keyed Will's car?"

"That was different," I protest. "He cheated on Londyn."

"*What?*" Payton shrieks. "I didn't know that. I wish you'd told me. I would've helped you keyed that fucker's car."

"Which is why we didn't tell you," I say, and Londyn nods in agreement.

Payton rolls her eyes as she slips her backpack on. "You're always trying to protect us."

"Yep," I say without shame. "And I'm trying to protect you when I say stay away from the neighbors."

After what she told me about the Porterson brothers, I'm even more desperate to keep my sisters away from them. Parentless. Troublemakers. Twins. Their family is practically the male version of ours, except I'd like to believe we're not quite as bad. I don't know how accurate that is. Over the years, my sisters and I have done our fair share of bad stuff, though I don't think people have ever referred to us as dangerous. Just trouble.

Still, put the eight of us together and it'll be the makings of a disaster.

"Wait, don't they have a sister?" I ask, recalling the girl who warned me about her brothers.

Payton nods, flipping her hair off her shoulder. "And she gets into just as much trouble as her brothers." Payton pops a piece of gum into her mouth. "You know what? Maybe I should see if I can dig up more dirt on them today, just so we know what to watch out for."

I shake my head. "Stay away from them. I mean it."

"Okay." But the mischievous glint in her eyes lets me know she's full of shit.

Sighing, I get out of the car, and my sisters follow. We start across the parking lot toward the entrance doors of the single-story, brick school. We're early, only a handful of students are around, but we somehow manage to draw attention.

"Why are they staring?" Londyn whispers. "Do I have toilet paper stuck to my shoe or something?"

I glance at her feet. "Nope. You're good."

"Maybe it's because we're new," Bailey suggests, glancing around the campus yard uneasily. "This is a small town. They probably know we're new."

"Maybe." But I have an unsettling feeling the dirty looks we're getting have nothing to do with our newbie status.

My doubt only escalates when we enter the school and the few people standing by their lockers start whispering and snickering in our direction.

Something is definitely going on, and I have a feeling it has to do with dipshit one, two, three, and four—yes, for now, I'm putting Rhyland in that category, too.

A second later, my suspicions are confirmed when I note the flyers taped to the lockers.

"What are those?" Bailey whispers, eyeballing them.

I pluck one off and start to read, anger rippling through me.

Everyone, I'd like to introduce you to the Harlyton sisters. They just moved here and will be joining our little student body population. The first thing you should know about them is they are quite the little kleptomaniacs. They can also be very manipulative. And according to some of their police records, they like to solve their problems with violence.

Below the note is a list of every crime my sisters and I have ever committed, along with a mugshot of Payton and Bailey, and yes, of me. Londyn is the only one of us who hasn't been arrested yet, but one of her yearbook photos is included. Even crimes never reported to the police are on there.

How did they learn all this?

Londyn leans over my shoulder to read it. "Wait. Is that a list of all the times we've gotten in trouble?"

Nodding, I crumple up the paper and begin ripping down the rest of them. We're early enough that maybe I can stop everyone from seeing them. Then again, the few people who already have seen them are more than likely going to gossip about it.

"Do you think the Porterson brothers did this?" Londyn hisses as she rushes after me while Payton takes off toward the bathroom.

"I'll go check on her," Bailey says, jogging after her.

I rip off more flyers and toss them into the trash can. "I don't *think* they did it. I *know* they did."

Londyn tears a flyer off a locker, her fingers slightly trembling. "How did they find all this dirt on us?"

I shrug, tearing a flyer in half. "I'm not sure." But I do know why they probably started searching for the info.

Back when I spoke to Rhyland, I accidentally let it

slip that my sisters got in trouble and sometimes even with the police.

This is all my fault.

I need to find a way to fix it, whatever it takes.

CHAPTER NINE

I'm a prideful person, have been for as long as I can remember. That pride can sometimes get me in trouble, like this whole ordeal with the Porterson brothers.

Maybe I should've just ignored Blaise's *baby* and *sweetheart* comments. That might have been easier. But ignoring isn't always necessarily the right thing to do, easier or not. And I'm sick of guys talking to me like I'm a ditzy girl who should just get all swoony because they glance my way or pay me a bit of attention when I don't even want it.

By the time I make it to first period English, I'm fuming mad. I haven't seen the Porterson brothers, but they have to be here, right? How else could those flyers have been put up?

"Fuck the Porterson brothers," I mutter as I slump

lower in my desk, waiting for the bell to ring while doing my best to ignore the gawks and whispers floating around me.

"Do you mean that literally?" Blaise's amused tone makes every single one of my muscles wind into knots. "Because, while that sounds interesting in theory, I'm not sure you can handle all four of us. Or even one of us."

I restlessly drum my fingers on top of my legs as I sense him take a seat in the desk behind mine. So many comebacks burn at the tip of my tongue, but I simmer them out, reigning back on my temper before turning around.

"Was it you?" I ask in an even tone.

He cocks his head to the side. "Was what me?"

I narrow my eyes at him. "Don't play dumb with me."

He slants forward, crossing his arms on his desk, his eyes swirling with a look that makes the air get caught in my lungs. "Then don't play dumb with me, sweetheart."

"Stop calling me sweetheart," I hiss. "And I'm not playing dumb."

"Yes, you were, by asking me if I did it instead of just accusing."

"Is that your way of confessing you put those flyers up all over the school?"

He works his jaw from side to side. "Confessing would mean I care. I don't."

My fingers fold inward. "I warned you to stay away from my sisters."

The corners of his lips kick up into a cold grin. "You really need to stop threatening me, sweetheart."

"And you need to stay away from me and my sisters." I lean in, my voice like ice. "And stop calling me sweetheart."

He rubs his lips together. "You know, most girls would love my attention."

I roll my eyes. "I highly doubt that."

He cocks a brow. "Don't believe me? Take a look around you."

I discreetly peer around and notice a few of the female population smiling at Blaise. And some dudes. "They're probably just staring in shock."

"About what?" His lips span into a grin. "My shocking good looks?"

"No, that someone so conceited actually exists."

He rolls his tongue in his mouth while restlessly tapping his pen against his desk. "You know, you've got quite a mouth on you, *sweetheart.*"

"And you've got quite a misconstrued self-perception, *small dick.*"

He nearly drops his pen. "Did you just call me *small dick?*"

"Yep, it's my new nickname for you. And I'm going to use it every time you call me anything else besides my name."

Blaise studies me with a mixture of curiosity and confusion. "I think—"

The bell rings, cutting him off. He appears pretty grateful for it.

Moments later, the teacher walks in, along with Jaxon, who hurriedly takes a seat in the desk across from Blaise's. His attempt to rush into class doesn't go unnoticed, as most of the people in the room sneak a glance at him. They do the same thing with Blaise. The more I observe the attention they're getting, the more I question if it isn't because of how good-looking there are, but because they're the town troublemakers.

As Jaxon pulls out his book, he offers me a coy smile, which I return with the dirtiest look I can muster.

His gaze nervously drops to his desk, which sort of makes me feel bad. Out of the four of them, Jaxon seems a bit shy. But I keep the apology to myself as the teacher announces the start of class.

I rotate around in my seat, putting my back to Blaise and Jaxon, and try not to think about any of the Porterson brothers.

When the teacher calls out my name, the entire class snickers.

My jaw ticks, and before I can even comprehend the consequences of my action, I kick my foot back and straight into Blaise's shin.

He groans, cursing under his breath. Then I feel him lean forward, his breath hot against my skin.

"So, you like it rough?" he whispers. "Good to know."

I shield my forehead with my hand as I lower my head, my cheeks flushing.

When his chuckle tickles my ear, I consider kicking him again, but after what he just said, I keep my feet glued to the ground, knowing reacting will give him more satisfaction than anything else.

No, if I want to get him back for outing my sisters' and my secrets, I'm going to have to find a non-violent way to do it.

And I will get my revenge.

Because no one messes with the Harlyton sisters and gets away with it.

CHAPTER TEN

When the bell rings, I gather my books and hurry out of class, taking the front exit instead of the back and running smack into a solid chest. To add to my embarrassment, I accidentally step on their toes and elbow them in the stomach.

"Sorry," I mutter, my gaze snapping up to meet Rhyland's gaze.

Great, out of all the people to run into.

The corners of his lips kick up into a half-smile. "It's okay. And I'm sorry, too."

"I don't know why you're apologizing." I shift my books in my arm. "I'm the one who ran into you."

"Yeah, but I wasn't really watching where I was going either." He offers me a charming smile.

I almost smile back until I note the abundance of

staring being aimed in our direction.

"Man, they don't let up, do they?" I mumble through a weighted sigh.

"Yeah, people around here have a bad habit of staring at my siblings and me." No arrogance is evident in his tone, just a simple matter of fact that he seems sort of sad about.

"I'm sure they do. But this time, I'm pretty sure they're staring at me." I turn around, ready to head to my next class and get the hell away from all the gawking.

"Wait." Rhyland jogs after me, tucking his books under his arm. "What did you mean by that?"

I throw him a *really* look. "Like you haven't heard the rumors."

He shakes his head. "I try to not listen to rumors, so no, I haven't."

I can't tell whether he's lying or not. "Maybe you should ask your brother then."

"My brother?" A crease etches between his brows. "Alex?"

"No, Blaise," I quicken my pace.

"Hadley, please just wait a minute." He captures my sleeve, and I grind to a halt. He waits for me to turn around before he says, "What do you mean I should ask Blaise?" He releases my sleeve. "Did he …?" He seems so lost. "Did he do something to you?"

I search his eyes, questioning if he's really as clueless as he's acting, but I don't know him well enough to determine that.

Huffing in frustration, I move over to the trash can, grab a flyer out of it, and slap it against Rhyland's chest. "Those were all over the school this morning, and I'm pretty sure Blaise was behind the prank. I also think maybe you had something to do with it since I told you about our … colorful past with the law."

He skims over the flyer, then his gaze elevates to mine. "I didn't have anything to do with this, I swear." He appears sincere, but again, I don't know him well enough to be certain. "And trust me; neither would Blaise."

I snort a laugh. "Okay, just like he didn't slash my tires."

His brows furrow. "But he didn't."

"Um, yeah, he did. He even said he did." I walk away, not wanting to hear any more of his lies.

Honestly, I can't blame him. If I were in his position and one of my sisters was getting accused of something like this, I'd lie for them, too.

And that's exactly why I hightail it toward the library. Because it's time to put a stop to this whole thing with the Porterson brothers. And I'll start by digging up some dirt on them, just like they did to us.

CHAPTER ELEVEN

Since I've used my data for the month and can't access the school's internet from my phone, I use the library computers to do a little bit of digging on the Portersons. When I type their names into the search engine, I get all sorts of hits, from petty theft to stealing a car. How they haven't been arrested yet is beyond me.

I also find out the names of their parents and their sister, Scarlett Porterson, who has gotten into just as much trouble and has spent some time in a psychiatric facility. She also has a different mom than Alex and Rhyland, and Blaise and Jaxon—guess Payton was right about their dad being a huge cheater—and she lives with her mom not too far away from our neighborhood.

Alex and Rhyland's mom has been in trouble with the law so many times she makes my dad look like a saint. And as for their dad, well, he's linked to many, many crimes in town, and a lot of charges are related to an illegal underground gambling club, yet somehow the guy has never been arrested.

Interesting. And maybe useful.

I continue to scroll through the information, trying to find out something about Blaise and Jaxon's mom, but I can't find much of anything, other than she was once married to their father, unlike Scarlett's mom and Alex and Rhyland's. Talk about a soap opera.

I'm so caught up in my research that I barely notice when the bell rings.

"Interesting research."

I jolt at the sound of Blaise's voice then quickly collect myself.

"Yeah, it's definitely interesting. I really like the part where Alex was arrested for drug trafficking." I spin the chair around to face him.

He's standing too close for comfort with a book in his hand, his expression guarded. "He wasn't arrested for that."

"That's not what his record says."

"Yeah, well, the charges were dropped."

"So what? He was still arrested."

"Over a misunderstanding," he stresses, shifting his weight uneasily.

So, his brothers are his weakness. I can understand that. Doesn't mean I'm going to go easy on him.

"Sure it was. Just like I'm sure the time he was arrested for stealing a car was a misunderstanding, too." I rise to my feet, collecting my bag from the back of the chair as the tardy bell rings.

Great. I'm late on the first day. Not a good start to a new school year.

He grinds his teeth, his gaze flicking from the computer to me. "How did you find out all that information anyway? Police records aren't supposed to be accessible to the public."

"Now, Blaise, let's not play dumb with each other after we've been so bluntly honest so far." I pat his arm then sling the handle of my bag over my shoulder. "After digging up all the dirt on my family, I'm sure you can figure that answer out for yourself."

He frowns. "Well, maybe I'm a little bit slow, so please enlighten me."

I shrug with a haughty grin. "Guess you'll never know then."

I swing around him, feeling pretty good about myself, even though I'm late to class. But seconds later, as I'm hurrying down an aisle of books, I trip over my own feet and knock several rows of books off the shelf, causing a scene.

Awesome.

I scramble to pick them up and shove them back on the shelves so I can get to class.

"Can I help you?" The librarian, a thirty-something-year-old woman, appears on the aisle beside me. She takes one look at the mess and frowns. "Don't just shove them all back on the shelves. There's a system to it." She crouches beside me and snatches the books from my hands.

"I'm sorry."

She slips a few books onto a shelf. "Shouldn't you be in class? Or do you have a pass? If you don't, I'm going to have to write you up for after school detention."

"I have a pass," I lie automatically.

Her skeptical gaze settles on me. "Can I see it?"

"Sure." I pretend to reach for my back pocket, preparing to haul ass out of there, figuring since I'm new here, it'll be really hard for her to figure out who I am, when a voice stops me.

"Hey, Ms. G., Hadley's actually helping me this period." Blaise materializes behind the librarian—Ms. G, I'm assuming.

Ms. G.'s eyelashes flutter as she cranes her neck to look up at Blaise. "Oh, I didn't know that. Thank you for letting me know."

"No problem." He dazzles her with a smile, not the smirk he's always throwing at me. "Do you need any help cleaning that up?"

She flashes him a flustered smile. "No, I think I got it. Thank you, though, for the offer. It's so nice of you."

"Anytime." He winks at her then scoops up a handful of books and places them on a shelf. Then he arches a brow at me, taunting amusement glittering in his eyes. "You coming?"

I don't want to accept his help. I want to run away or simply declare I'm ditching. But my desire not to get detention wins.

Nodding, I rise to my feet. "Yeah."

Flashing me a toothy grin, he nods for me to follow him out of the library.

Once we make it into the hallway, I turn to head in the opposite direction as him, but he skitters in my path, nearly sending me tripping over my feet.

"You know, most people would thank me for coming to their rescue," he says, crossing his arms.

"You didn't come to my rescue," I retort. "I totally had that handled before you showed up and flirted with poor Ms. G."

His lips kick up into a half-smile. "She didn't seem to mind."

"So? That doesn't make it right."

A smug smile plays at the corners of his lips. "Are you jealous?"

A snort escapes me. "Oh, my God, are you being serious right now?"

"You know, it's been a long time since someone laughed in my face." His tone is low, but not threatening, just confused.

"That you know of."

"The term laughed in my face means that I'd know, since the act has to be done right in front of me."

Okay, he has me there, but I'm not about to lose this battle. "I don't know. Maybe they did laugh in your face, but you were too busy staring in a mirror, admiring your own reflection, to notice."

His brow rises. "Are you saying I'm vain?"

I give a half-shrug. "You do seem to like yourself a lot."

Tracing the tip of his tongue along his lips, he dips his head toward my ear. "You owe me now. You do realize that, right?"

I put my lips beside his ear, throwing his move right back at him. "You slit my car's tires, disassembled the carburetor, then basically showed the entire school my family's entire rap sheet. I'm far from ever owing you anything."

He leans back, his lips parting then closing. Then his expression hardens. "If you want to go up against the big boys, you should know what you're getting into." He lowers his voice. "The Portersons have all sorts of connections around town, and we know everything about everyone. Remember that when you're trying to get back at me and my brothers." With that, he turns around and swaggers off like he's the fucking shit in this town. And maybe he is now, but when I get done with him, he sure as hell won't be.

CHAPTER TWELVE

RHYLAND AND JAXON ARE IN MY NEXT TWO CLASSES. Rhyland tries to strike up a conversation with me a couple times, but he quickly gives up when I give him the cold shoulder.

When I try to make small chitchat with a couple of people outside the Porterson clan, figuring it might be good to have some friends—or allies—I get snubbed and laughed at. The only person who acknowledges my existence is Scarlett.

"Sorry, but I tried to warn you not to go up against them," she says as we pass each other in the hallway.

"I didn't really go up against them," I point out. "Well, not until about an hour ago." When Blaise found me looking up information about his family.

The only reason I knew how to access most of those records is because of my dad. There's no way I'll ever tell Blaise that. Although, I'm surprised he couldn't figure it out on his own. I mean, after digging up all that dirt on my family, he has to know my dad used to work as a detective.

"Why? What happened an hour ago?" she asks, intrigued.

"I'm sure Blaise will tell you all about it." I'm surprised he hasn't already.

"My brothers don't really tell me much about their extracurricular activities." She pulls out a package of M&Ms from her bag and pops a handful into her mouth, then offers me some.

Even though the motive behind Scarlett's friendliness is questionable, I'm hungry, so I take a handful and pop them into my mouth.

"So, torturing me and my sisters is considered an extracurricular activity for your brothers?" I ask as she stuffs the candy back into her bag.

She chuckles. "For now, I guess it is. Don't worry, though; Blaise will get it under control eventually."

"You say that like he has no control over his own actions."

"No, he does. It's my brothers' actions he has a hard time controlling." She throws me a wave as she turns to leave. "See you around, Hadley. And if this thing with my brothers ever ends, we should hang out sometime. I don't have many friends, mostly since the people around here are afraid of my brothers. You don't seem to have that problem, though."

I think about what I read about her. How she spent some time in a psychiatric ward. I couldn't find out why. Doesn't really matter, though. She seems nice enough, unlike her brothers.

"Yeah, if that ever happens, we should definitely hang out." I smile at her as I start to turn for my next class.

"If you really want to end this feud quicker, you could always challenge one of them," she calls out, stopping me in my tracks.

I twist back around, ignoring the group of cheerleaders laughing at me from just down the busy hallway. "What do you mean by challenge? Challenge them to what?"

She adjusts her backpack with a smile on her face. A smile that is either extremely genuine or creepily malicious—she's very hard to read.

"A drag race." She hitches her thumbs around the handles of her backpack and shrugs. "It's sort of a thing in Honeyton."

"Drag racing?"

"A drag race duel."

I'm unsure what to make of this, and she must read the confusion on my face because she adds, "Okay, so let's say Nina over there"—she gestures at a brown-haired girl standing amongst the group of cheerleaders—"has a thing for jock head number one"—she points at a blond-haired guy standing next to the brown-haired girl—"and jock head number two." She points to the guy standing next to him. "And she ends up sleeping with them both, and they both find out. And for some dumb reason, they start fighting over her. Instead of beating each other's asses, they declare a racing duel. Winner gets Nina's heart forever." She pulls a look of disgust.

I cock a brow. "That's really a thing?"

"Well, not the whole thing about Nina and jock head one and two. I was just giving you an example. But yes, in this hick town you've decided to declare your new home, we sometimes settle our lame-ass problems with racing."

I mull over the idea. While a drag race duel seems a bit strange and old-school, getting Blaise to back off is appealing. Plus, I'd get a lot of satisfaction in beating his ass in a race. On the other hand, he slit my tires and showed the entire school my family's fucked-up history, and winning against him in a race doesn't seem like much of a payback.

"Just think about it," Scarlett says then walks off as

the bell rings, announcing that yes, once again, I'm late to class.

Needless to say, by lunchtime, I'm pretty tired of the day. So, when I meet up with my sisters at my locker and Londyn and Bailey inform me that Payton went home before school even started, I volunteer to go check on her.

"Are you sure?" Londyn double-checks as I put my stuff in my bag. "I don't think it's a good idea to miss half a day on our first day of school."

"I'll be fine," I assure her as I bump my locker shut. "It's not like I've never missed a first day of school before."

"Yeah, but it doesn't mean you should continually do it either." Londyn walks down the hallway beside me with Bailey trailing at our heels.

Londyn's right, but that doesn't mean I'm not going to do it. I don't like that Payton is home alone and upset. Or worse, what if she isn't home alone because our dad came home drunk?

"I'll see if I can coax her into coming back," I tell Londyn as we reach the exit. "I'll text you if we do. If not, I'll pick you guys up when school gets out."

Sighing, Londyn steps back. "Fine. But I'm really starting to hate the Porterson brothers."

"Me, too," I agree, thinking about how the duel

could end this. Either that or I could get over my pride and let what Blaise did go.

"Give Payton a hug for me," Bailey says. "She was really upset when she took off … Those flyers … They said a lot of bad stuff about her—about all of us."

"I'll give her ten hugs," I promise, then wave goodbye and push out the doors.

The drive home should take about ten minutes, but I manage to make it in seven by speeding and cutting corners. By the time I pull up, I'm fuming mad. Not at Payton. No, I can understand why she was upset and took off. She has one of the worst reps out of the four of us, and that flyer basically declared her a kleptomaniac.

I'm mad at Blaise Porterson.

I don't give a shit if he bailed me out of getting detention. He never should've messed with my sisters.

My rage only simmers hotter when I find Payton locked in her bedroom.

"Go away!" she shouts through a sob.

I knock softly on the door. "Come on, Payton. You're stronger than this."

"No, I'm not," she cries out. "Just leave me alone!" She then cranks the music up, the walls vibrating with the bass.

I consider picking the lock, but I decide to give her a bit of time to wallow before I go that far. Instead, I send

Londyn and Bailey a text that Payton and I aren't returning to school today. Then I trudge to my room and work on bottling up my pride while I wait.

Wait until it's time to go pick up my sisters. Then I'll declare a duel and hopefully put an end to this battle with the Porterson brothers that's making our lives a living hell.

CHAPTER THIRTEEN

I decide to clean the house while I wait, though I hate cleaning. But the empty boxes cluttering up the house are starting to drive me crazy.

I've just finished up and am collecting my car keys to head back to pick up Bailey and Londyn when I hear the grumbling of an engine outside. Peering out the window, I spot my dad's truck parked in the driveway.

He hops out with a duffel bag slung over his shoulder and peers around sketchily before rushing up the driveway and ducking into the garage/shed.

"Just what are you up to, Dad?" I debate on whether to go out and ask or spy on him.

Since going out and asking gives him the opportunity to lie, I decide spying is the better choice, so I wait by the window and watch.

After being in the garage/shed for only a minute or two, he hurries back outside with a shovel and makes a beeline for the backyard. I scramble to the washroom where the window gives me a better view of the area.

Confusion instantly sets in as I watch him start to dig a hole near the back fence. He doesn't dig for very long before dropping the duffel bag into the hole. Then he covers it up with dirt, returns the shovel to the garage/shed, gets in his car, and takes off down the road in the direction he drove off in last week.

I'm about to go out and see what the hell is in the bag—because whatever it is, it can't be good—when I receive a text from Londyn.

Londyn: Are you coming to get us? I'd really like to get away from this place ASAP.

Realizing I'm late, I bail on digging up the bag. For now anyway. The second I return home, however, I'm so finding out.

Before I leave, I knock on Payton's door and ask her if she wants to go with me.

"I'm never going back there *ever*!" she shouts.

I sigh. "You know you're going to have to eventually."

I sigh again when she doesn't respond.

Resting my forehead against the door, I blow out a breath. "Just come with me please. I'm only pulling into the parking lot. You don't even have to get out of the car."

When silence is my only response, I give up and start to back away when the door swings open and Payton moves into the doorway.

"Fine, I'll go. But we're stopping at the gas station and getting me a soda on the way back."

I nod, relieved but trying not to show it, knowing she'll just get upset again. "All right, sounds like a plan."

Nodding, she brushes past me and starts down the stairs.

"Hey, did you by chance notice Dad burying a duffel bag in the backyard?" I ask as I follow after her.

She shakes her head as she steps into the kitchen. "No. Why?"

I shrug. "Because he did."

She opens the door and steps outside, casting a quick glance over her shoulder at me. "What was in the bag?"

I close the door and lock it up. "I have no idea."

A beat of silence passes as our gazes drift to the backyard.

"We should probably go look and see, right?" She returns her gaze to me as she walks up to my car and pulls open the passenger side door to get in.

I nod, digging the keys out of my pocket. "Definitely. But we need to pick up Londyn and Bailey first."

"I can't believe they stuck it out today," she mumbles after we get in the car.

I slip the keys into the ignition and start up the engine. "I know you might not want to hear this, but eventually you're going to have to go to school. And I'd prefer for that to be sooner than later." I shift into reverse. "I don't like the idea of you being home alone if Dad's going to be burying bags in the backyard."

She fastens her seatbelt. "What do you think is in it?"

I shrug as I steer down the road. "Drug money? Drugs? When it comes to him, nothing surprises me anymore."

Her eyes widen. "You think Dad's doing drugs?"

I already know he does, but she doesn't need to know that.

"Probably not," I reply evasively. "Maybe I'm overreacting. Maybe whatever's in the bag has something to do with his work." My naïve words are more of an attempt to alleviate her worry than anything else.

"What sort of job requires an employee to bury duffel bags in their backyard?"

"I don't know."

She stares at me accusingly. "You don't know? Or you don't want to say?"

While I have no clue what my dad is doing for work, or if he even really has a job, if he's burying duffel bags in the backyard at three o'clock in the afternoon, I'm sure it's not a good job. But telling her this will only make her worry, and she already has her own issues to deal with right now.

I internally breathe in relief when we turn into the school parking lot, latching on to the distraction. "Do you see them anywhere?"

She sits up and scans the parking area for our sisters. Since we're late, most of the cars have thinned out.

"Um, Hadley?" Worry rings in Payton's tone.

I track her gaze and quickly figure out why.

Parked near the front entrance is the Portersons' SUV. And standing beside it is Alex and Jaxon, along with Londyn and Bailey. And man, do they look pissed off.

"Shit." I pull my car up behind their SUV, silence the engine, and hop out.

"So, you're saying what was on the flyers isn't true?" Alex is saying—or more like taunting—as I approach them.

"I'm pretty sure you already know it is," Londyn bites out, stepping toward him, "since you and your brothers are the ones who put them up."

Alex's lips pull into a smirk. "Then, why are we even talking about this? I mean, if you know we did it and the flyers are true?"

Londyn lowers her arms to her sides, her hands clenched into fists. "Because you guys shouldn't have done it!" Her voice echoes across the parking lot. Bailey's eyes widen. So do mine.

Never have I seen Londyn get so upset, at least not in public.

"Is there a problem?" I interrupt, strolling up and getting in Alex's personal space, totally on purpose.

He's tall—all of the Porterson brothers are—and even at my five-foot-nine frame, I have to angle my chin up to meet his gaze, which is annoying. He looks strung out, like he spent all of yesterday high and is now worn out. Well, either that or he slept like shit.

His narrowed eyes land on me. "Yeah, your sister here"—he nods at Londyn—"needs to learn her place."

I raise my brows. "And what place would that be?"

His gaze dances back and forth between us, a smile playing at his lips. Beneath the arrogance, I detect the slightest bit of uncertainty. Not sure why, but I'd love to find out. Find out why these guys are so set on pissing my sisters and me off. Although, Jaxon doesn't seem to be part of the battle, standing a ways back, his shoulders slumped, his mouth set in a deep frown. But just because he's a bystander, that doesn't make him any better.

"The place where she realizes who owns this town." Alex slants into my face, his smirk appearing.

Holding my ground, I refuse to cower back. "I'm pretty sure the mayor owns this town."

He rolls his eyes. "You're so fucking clueless."

"And you're a dickless jerk," I snap. "And a hypocrite."

A crease forms between his brows. "How the hell am I a hypocrite?"

I inch closer to him, getting in his face like he did mine. "You and your brothers posted all those flyers around school that told everyone about our shady backgrounds as if we're these horrible criminals. And yet, your family's track record is just as sketchy." I point a finger at him. "In fact, yours is probably the worst." I put on a smile, but it's anything but friendly. "Maybe we should even out the playing grounds and let everyone in school know your family is right up there with ours."

He laughs hollowly. "Like I give a shit. Everyone already knows anyway. And even if it was new information, no one would dare do anything to us. People respect us too much around here."

I lift a brow. "Do they respect you? Or are they afraid of you?"

His lips span back into a smirk. "Isn't fear and respect the same thing?"

What a misconstrued logic he has.

"If you really believe that, then I pity you."

Irritation flashes in his eyes, and I realize I hit a sore subject. Good. I hope he's annoyed.

His voice descends a notch. "Maybe you need to learn your place in this town, too."

"I already know it," I smart back. "It's right here, handing your ass to you, dude."

A muscle in his jaw spasms as his lips part. Who knows what foul words he would've thrown in my face if Rhyland and Blaise weren't strolling up at that precise moment.

"What's going on?" Blaise halts to the side of us, his gaze shifting back and forth between Alex and me.

This situation probably seems a bit odd, considering we're standing almost close enough to kiss.

"Oh, nothing." I put a drop of space between Alex and me. "Your brother was just trying to tell me where my place is in this town."

Blaise blasts Alex with a hard look, but Alex only shrugs.

Grinding his teeth from side to side, Blaise fixes his gaze on me. Before he can utter a word, though, I hold up my hand.

"Look, I don't want to argue anymore, okay? It's not my MO."

Blaise's lips twitch. "Yeah, I have a hard time believing that."

"Don't pretend like you have any insight into me

just because you dug up my criminal history." I turn to face him, crossing my arms. "You know nothing about me or my past, and you had no right to put up those flyers."

Blaise frowns. "Maybe you're right, but we still did it."

Rhyland shakes his head with severe annoyance. "Don't drag me into this shit." He locks gazes with me. "Hadley, I had nothing to do with the flyers, and I hope you won't hold it against me."

"I didn't either," Jaxon chimes in, reclining against the side of the SUV.

Alex rolls his eyes while Blaise pinches the brim of his nose. I take their silence as guilty admittance, minus the guilt.

"I don't really care which one of you did it," I declare. "I just want all of you to leave me and my sisters alone." I pause, hoping to God that Scarlett wasn't screwing around with me when she told me about the duel thing. "So, I'm declaring a drag racing duel."

"What the hell is that?" Londyn mumbles from behind me.

"I have no idea," Bailey whispers. "But it sounds intriguing."

Blaise's hand falls to his side, his eyes sparkling with a hint of surprise. "How did you find out about that?"

"Because I'm pretty sure no one talked to you the entire day," Alex adds, staring me down hard.

"Now, why would I out my only friend here?" I smile as their puzzlement grows. "So, do you accept the challenge or not?"

Blaise observes me cautiously. "Which one of us are you challenging?"

I offer him the same smirk he's thrown at me time and time again. "Why you, of course, *sweetheart*." While kicking Alex's ass in a race does sound appealing, Blaise has pissed me off more.

His intense gaze bores into me, the corners of his lips twitching as he leans closer. "You don't know what you're getting yourself into," he whispers softly. "You should back out now before you get in too deep."

"Is that a threat?" I whisper back hotly.

"No, I'm trying to help you. You don't want to get messed up in our drama." He skims a finger along my wrist, causing me to jolt and my heart to skip a beat.

Why the hell did he touch me like that? To mess with my head probably.

I lift my hand to shove him away, but he steps back on his own.

"If you want to duel, then we can duel. But I'm warning you, you're not going to win." His gaze strays to my car. "Not in that."

All I do is shrug. While my car looks like a piece of

shit on the outside, it runs pretty smoothly. If he knew anything about cars, he would know that, especially if he helped disassemble the carburetor. Seeing as he doesn't seem aware of what's hidden underneath that hood, my guess is he's pretty clueless about cars and doesn't spend a whole lot of time drag racing.

That thought makes me smile, which Blaise more than notices.

"You do realize Rhyland has never lost a race ever and Alex is a mechanic, right?" he tells me almost apologetically.

My brow quirks upward. "Did I challenge them to a race?"

He exhales loudly. "Fine, but don't say I didn't warn you."

"And don't say I didn't warn you when you get your ass kicked."

He rubs his forehead and sighs. "So, what're the terms of the race? I mean, what do I get if I win?" He dazzles me with his pearly whites when I glare at him.

Then I mirror his smirk. "Well, when *I* win, you and your brothers will leave my sisters and me alone. No more flyers. No more messing up my car. No more doing anything that makes our lives even the slightest bit complicated, got it?"

He tilts his head to the side, considering. "That sounds doable, I guess."

Alex snorts a laugh. "Don't agree for all of us."

Blaise shoots him a warning look then looks back at me. "If you win, I promise *all* of us will leave you and your sisters alone. But when *I* win"—his lips quirk as I glower at him—"you owe me a month's worth of favors. Anything I ask for, you do."

I promptly shake my head. "Anything is too broad of a word."

He wavers. "Okay, I promise none of the favors will be dangerous or will require you to do anything that'd get you hurt."

I don't want to say what's biting at the tip of my tongue, since it will probably get laughed at when I do, but it needs to be said. "Nothing sexual either." I give myself a pat on the back for my even tone.

Blaise slips his tongue out, wetting his lips, amusement dancing in his eyes. "The last thing I'd ever want is for you to give me sexual favors." My lips part with a comeback, when he leans closer and whispers, "When stuff finally does happen between us, it'll happen because you want it."

My blood burns beneath my skin. "And to think, you were just starting to seem not as annoying as when I first met you."

He chuckles softly. "You know what? I take back what I said. I do want you to kiss me when I win."

I slant back and glare at him. "I already said no sexual favors."

"It won't be a favor. Just an extra prize." He's all grins and wickedness. "Just one kiss, and then you can spend the next month reliving it over and over in your memory."

"You mean my nightmares."

"Are you afraid you'll lose? It sure sounds like you are."

Fuck. I'm not sure what to do. On the one hand, I doubt I'll lose. But what if I do? Then I'd have to kiss this asshat and do a bunch of favors for him, which possibly means spending time with him. On the other hand, backing down now is going to make me seem weak. Plus, if I win, they'll have to leave my sisters and me alone.

"Fine," I say. "But I want an extra prize, too."

His smile radiates amusement. "All right, what is it?"

A Cheshire grin spreads across my lips. "I get to kick you in the balls."

His smile falters. "No fucking way."

I sniff the air. "Is that fear I smell?"

His eyes narrow into slits. "Being afraid would mean I think I'm going to lose. I'm not."

I shrug, still smirking. "Then I guess we don't have a problem."

He smirks back. "I guess we don't."

We stare each other down hard until someone clears their throat, startling us both, as if we forgot other people are here.

Raking his hands through his hair, Blaise steps away from me. "All right, you want a duel, then let's duel." He digs his keys out of his pocket. "Meet me at the turnout in twenty minutes. I have to pick up Rhyland's car first."

"Okay." Even though I'm clueless as to where the turnout is, I don't give him the satisfaction of asking. I also try not to reveal my panic over the mention of Rhyland's car.

Through all the smack talk, I forgot about Rhyland's awesome ride and didn't take a moment to consider how Blaise would more than likely race it.

Blaise pauses, observing me. "You have a problem with my ride?"

"Nope." When I return his obsessive stare, he grins then climbs into the SUV.

Rhyland turns to me, sighing heavily. "Are you sure you know what you're getting into?"

"You're the one who suggested I start racing in this town," I remind him, tucking a strand of hair behind my ear.

"I know, but ..." A frown etches into his face. "I'm not sure you fully understand what you're getting into."

I shrug. "Doesn't really matter since I'm not going to lose."

His frown deepens, then he shakes his head and slips into the front seat of the SUV while Jaxon clambers into the back seat.

Alex makes no move to get in, smirking at me instead. "You're going down. You do realize that, right?"

Smiling sweetly, I pat him on the shoulder. "I guess we should say our goodbyes now, right? Since soon you're going to have to leave us alone. Although, I don't even know why you are bothering us to begin with."

"I have my reasons," he sneers, then gives me a pat on the arm. "And just know that, when you lose, I'm going to add a list of favors of my own to Blaise's list. So, have fun with that." Then he turns and hops into the back seat.

Shaking my head, I hurriedly usher my sisters into my own car where Payton is waiting.

"What's going on?" she asks the instant we hop in.

I rev up the engine. "I'm getting us off the Porterson brothers' radar.

"Well, either that, or you're putting yourself on their radar even more." Londyn violently fastens her seatbelt. "What were you thinking, Hadley? Agreeing to do Blaise favors? And to kiss him!"

"*What?*" Payton cries, her eyes huge.

"I was thinking that I rarely lose a race, so none of that's going to be a problem." I push on the gas and drive forward.

Londyn huffs an exasperated breath. "You're always putting us first, and this time, I think you've gone too far."

"Doesn't really matter what you think." I offer an apologetic look. "What's done is done."

"And if you lose?" she asks, giving me a pressing look. "Then what?"

"I won't lose," I stress, crossing my fingers that I'm right.

If not, my life is going to get a hell of a lot more complicated. And considering my dad just buried a bag of who knows what in the backyard, the last thing I need is more complications.

CHAPTER FOURTEEN

I stop at a gas station and ask for directions to the turnout. It must be a pretty popular place since the clerk knows exactly where it is. The area isn't too far away, just outside of town near the foothills.

During the drive there, we explain to Payton what happened. Confliction masks her face, as if she doesn't know whether to be happy about the duel or worried.

"Don't worry; I'll win," I assure her as I pull into the turnout, a flattened-out spot right next to the road.

"But, what if you don't?" Payton asks, slipping on a pair of oversized sunglasses. "Then you'll end up spending the next month doing them awful favors."

"We don't know for sure that they'll be awful," I say, quieting the engine.

"Um, yeah, we do," Bailey tells me. "Those guys are straight-up evil."

"Nothing will be bad. Remember the stipulations I made?" I shove open the door and stretch my legs as I get out of the car.

"There're always loopholes," Bailey says as I slant the seat forward to let her out.

"Stop talking as if I'm going to lose, because I'm not." I plaster on a cocky grin, but it's all bravado. "Now, get out so I can win a race."

Bailey swiftly shakes her head. "No way. You're not doing this alone."

"You have to get out." I glance at all of them. "You all do."

Londyn's mouth sinks into a frown. "We're not letting you do this alone."

"It's not about doing this alone." Not entirely anyway. "It's about the extra weight in the car." And how this road runs alongside a shallow cliff that bottoms out into a river.

Londyn's lips form an *O*. Then she begrudgingly drags her butt out of the car, Payton and Bailey following. By the time they've gotten out, Rhyland's GTO is pulling into the turnout.

Blaise pulls up to the side of me and rolls the window down. "I see you found the place."

I slant against my car and cross my arms. "It wasn't that hard to find."

He grins. "Yeah, but I thought maybe you'd use getting lost as an excuse."

I push away from the car, lean down, rest my arms on the windowsill, and level my gaze with his. "You don't scare me."

He sinks his teeth into his bottom lip, his amusement doubling. "We'll see if you can still say that when you lose."

I step back and flip him off, which only elicits a chuckle from him.

"So, where are we racing to? And where are we lining up?"

"We'll turn around near that rock up there." He points at a large rock on the side of the road, just a ways up, then nods his head at the passenger seat where Rhyland is sitting. "And he'll line us up."

That's when I become aware that Jaxon and Alex aren't with them.

"Where're the rest of your demon squad?" I ask as Rhyland gets out of the car.

"I told them they couldn't come." Blaise slips on a pair of sunglasses. "Figured I'd do you a solid and let less people witness your ass getting kicked."

"Or, did you just not want them to see *your* ass getting kicked?" I quip haughtily.

He rolls his tongue in his mouth, struggling not to smile. "You're a fucking handful, aren't you? Seriously, how many times has your mouth gotten you in trouble?"

"More than I can count," I admit truthfully. "But I can always handle whatever comes my way, even cocky, pretty boy assholes."

He straightens, slipping his sunglasses down the brim of his nose. "Did you just call me a pretty boy?"

I shrug innocently. "The name seems pretty fitting. Do you prefer my other nicknames instead?"

"You can call me anything you want for now, sweetheart." His lips tug into a grin. "But when I win, I want you to call me *master*. In fact, it can be my first favor."

"I'm going to love watching your face twist in pain when I slam your man goodies with the tip of my boot." I leave it at that and hike back to my car, ignoring his chuckles as I slide into the torn leather seat of my car.

"Are we ready to do this?" Rhyland shouts as he moves to the center of the road.

Londyn ushers Payton and Bailey to the side and into the shade of the trees as I shift the car into drive and pull forward to where Rhyland is standing.

After Blaise and I line up, I crank up some music, tuning out the outside world as best as I can. Then I stare straight ahead at the desolate road in front of me that stretches between the cliff side.

Most of the races I've participated in have taken place on back roads that I've driven on before. This road is new to me, which gives me a disadvantage, but I try not to think too much about that as Rhyland raises his arms in the air.

"On your mark," Rhyland starts. "Get set, go!" He drops his arms, and then the squealing of tires floods the air as Blaise and I peel out.

I focus on the road ahead as I speed up, only measuring where Blaise is a couple times. Every time I look his way, he's right beside me. That's okay. I'm awesome at turn arounds and figure that's where I'll lose him.

As I approach the rock, I don't slow down, but speed up instead. Blaise must hesitate because his car slides out of my view. I mentally give myself a high-five then shove all thoughts aside and focus. I'm approaching the rock fast. If I don't do this just right, I'm going to end up skidding off course, or worse, off the road and into the river.

Just like Mom.

My heart skips a beat at the thought, and my hands begin to sweat.

"Come on, come on, come on," I chant as I grip the wheel. "Keep your shit together, Hadley. Don't let your head go there."

When the front end of my nose passes the rock, I

press on the brake and crank the wheel. The timing is perfect, and the turn would've been, too, if my tires didn't hit a patch of gravel and I started to skid.

For a faltering, heart terrifying moment, I'm a little girl again, standing on the side of the road, watching as my mom loses control of her car.

My heart races as I slowly let the car straighten out to avoid overcorrecting. Only when I regain control again does my heart settle down.

Letting out a shaky breath, I press on the gas. The skidding incident has shaved off some of my lead, and by the time I start racing toward the finish line, Rhyland and I are side by side again.

Refusing to lose, I slam my foot down on the gas pedal. The engine roars as I push the car faster, gripping the wheel tighter, determined to win.

"Come on, come on, come—" I zoom past the finish line, and so does Blaise. "Shit."

I slow down, knowing the race was close. So close that I'm not one hundred percent confident I won. That doesn't mean I'm not going to fake it.

I turn around and park on the side of the road near my sisters, then jump out of the car with a huge-ass grin on my face. Deep down inside, though, I'm a bit shaky, not just over losing, but over momentarily losing control of my car near a river.

I quickly shake my jitteriness off as Blaise gets out of his car.

"What're you smiling about?" Blaise asks. "Because you get to kiss me?"

"No, because I totally won that race," I scoff. "Now get over here so my boot can get acquainted with your balls."

He shakes his head, coming to a stop in front of me, and draws off his sunglasses. "No way. I'm the winner, so pucker up."

Rhyland joins Blaise's side with his phone in hand. "Actually, I think it might've been a tie."

Blaise and I simultaneously gape at him and say, "A tie?"

Rhyland holds up his phone. On the screen is a shot of Blaise and I crossing the finish line at the exact same time.

Londyn moves up to my side, with Bailey and Payton right behind her. "So, I guess you both lose then."

"Or both win," Blaise suggest, glancing at me.

I grimace over my two options. Either I can declare us both losers and no one wins anything, or I agree we're both winners, get assurance that the Porterson brothers will leave my sisters alone, and get to kick Blaise in the junk. But that also means I'll owe him a month's worth of favors and a kiss.

While the idea of doing Blaise favors makes me want to vagina punch myself, I want my sisters to have peace of mind during our time in Honeyton.

I blow out an exasperated exhale. "Fine, we're both winners."

A trace of a smile touches Blaise's lips. "All right then. My brothers and I won't bother your sisters anymore. Just make sure to be at my house at seven o'clock on the dot tomorrow morning to do my first favor." He starts to turn away and, for the stupidest moment, I wonder if perhaps he either forgot about the kiss or was only joking about it. But then he makes a U-turn. "Oh yeah, I almost forgot about the second part of our deal."

He stops in front of me and cups the back of my neck. I want to spit out excuses, protest, but backing down isn't my thing. So, I do the only thing I can. I kiss him first, not letting him have any sort of gratification in this.

Or, well, that's what I tell myself. But the moment our lips connect and he's kissing me—and I mean, *really* kissing me, his tongue parting my lips as he angles my head back and kisses me deeply—I nearly groan as warmth spreads throughout my body, a mixture of angsty lust and fuming irritation.

I'm enjoying kissing Blaise. What the hell is wrong with me?

Snapping out of my brief trance, I jerk back, gasping for air.

His eyelids flutter open, and the heated look he gives me makes me want to kiss him again. But then that stupid infamous smirk of his appears and any desire I felt fizzles.

"You pulled away first," he says, like that means I lost a battle.

I kind of feel like I did.

I need to get my shit together.

"Yep, I sure did. But only to do this." I kick him between the legs.

He grunts, crouching over in pain.

"Shit, you're ruthless," Rhyland mumbles, shaking his head as he gapes at me.

"Remember that." I point at him then focus back on Blaise, who is hunched over and red-faced, clutching his man goodies. "I'll see you bright and early tomorrow morning, sweetheart." Then I reel around and get in the car, telling myself that I'm okay. That I can handle this. That I can handle tomorrow. That I can handle anything.

"Are you okay?" Londyn asks me the second we are all in the car.

"Yep, just peachy," I lie as I steer away from the turnout.

Londyn assesses me with a disbelieving frown. She

knows me too well. "You lost control of the car there for a second."

"It scared me," Bailey whispers from the back seat.

I grip the steering wheel. "I had it under control." *Liar.* For a split-second, I thought I was going to skid off the road. And then what? I'd be gone and my sisters would be left with my father?

But isn't that what I'm going to do anyway when I take off to college?

I swallow hard, guilt creeping up on me.

Silence trickles by as I steer out onto the road, my guilt and the tension in the car growing with every mile marker we pass.

"Well, on the bright side, at least the kiss was hot," Payton finally breaks the tense silence.

I can't help smiling. At least one thing came out of this ordeal. She'd been so down when we left the house earlier, but now she seems upbeat again.

"It wasn't hot," I lie. "It was disgusting."

"If you say so." Payton snickers, and so does Bailey.

I want to protest, but the truth is, the kiss was hot. Scorching even.

I'm seriously disgusted with myself right now.

Londyn's expression fills with sympathy. "It's okay to like the kiss, Had. It doesn't mean you like him."

"I didn't like the kiss," I lie again, frustrated I'm not hiding my feelings very well.

"Okay." She squeezes my hand. A pity squeeze, I'm sure. Then she retrieves her phone and checks her texts, giggling at something on the screen.

Bailey and Payton start chatting in the back seat, Bailey telling Payton about all the cute boys she saw in school and how there was a flyer for an afterschool art program that Payton should totally check out.

Their laughter and smiles make whatever tomorrow holds, good or bad—but I'm positive it's going to be bad —worth it.

CHAPTER FIFTEEN

By the time we get home, the sun is setting behind the hills and my head is still stuck in worry mode over tomorrow morning. Since Dad isn't home yet, I decide to take the opportunity to distract my worried thoughts by digging up the bag he buried.

Through all the chaos of the duel, Payton and I forgot to mention the bag incident to Bailey and Londyn, which is a good thing. It gives me time to see what's in it so I can decide whether to keep it a secret or not.

After double-checking that my sisters are all busy and distracted, I slip outside and into the garage/shed to grab the shovel. As I'm headed back out, though, I pause as I hear Blaise and Alex talking nearby.

"You have to back off," Blaise hisses. "I made a deal with her."

"Yeah, so what? I didn't," Alex retorts. "And you should've talked to all of us first before you decided on the terms of that bet."

"The terms aren't a bad thing," Blaise replies lowly. "You need to leave the Harlyton sisters alone anyway now that their dad is working for ours."

Wait. My dad is working for their dad? The man who, from the research I found online, owns a bunch of illegal underground gambling clubs?

I shake my head. *Nice job choice, Dad.*

Alex laughs darkly. "Don't even get me started on that."

"Is that what this is about?" Blaise asks, sounding astounded. "Because, if so, you need to get over it."

"I'm not going to get over it," Alex growls out. "And you shouldn't either. He fucked us over."

Huh? Who fucked them over? Their dad or mine?

No, that doesn't make sense. We've barely lived here a little over a week. Then again, it wouldn't be the first time my dad's managed to piss someone off so quickly.

"Hadley and her sisters have nothing to do with that, so leave them alone," Blaise warns. "No more slitting tires, no more flyers, and no more harassing our new neighbors, got it? I'm sick of taking the blame for the shit you do."

"You don't have to do it," Alex mumbles.

"Yes, I do. If I didn't, you would've been in juvie by now. And if you keep it up, Social Services is going to get called. And Jaxon's still young enough to get taken away."

"Is that why you're so pissed off? Because I keep fucking up? Or are you pissed because I ruined your chances with Hadley?"

"I never wanted a chance with Hadley," Blaise replies flatly. "Stop assuming shit."

Alex snorts a laugh. "You so do. It's why you bought her new tires and added that kiss to the stupid bet. I know you, bro. You want her."

"That's not why I did any of that," Blaise snaps. "Now get in the car. It's time to go."

Doors slam then an engine roars to life. A few heartbeats later, the air grows silent again.

I leave the garage/shed, a bit shocked at what I heard. Not just the part about my dad working for theirs, but that Blaise was behind my brand-new tires and that he didn't slit them, nor did he put up the flyers. The gesture would've been nice if his brother hadn't damaged the tires and put those flyers all over school to begin with.

Still, as I dig up the bag, I wonder if my first impression of Blaise was wrong. Perhaps he's a decent guy, just a bit cocky and our personalities clash. A lot.

Of course, when I get the bag out of the ground and unzipped, I realize I have bigger problems than whether Blaise is really a douchebag or not.

"Fuck," I mutter as I peer into the bag that's stuffed with a huge stash of money and a brick of what looks like cocaine.

"Holy shit, Dad," I mumble as I shine the light of my phone into the inside of the bag. "Where the hell did you get all this?"

My mind is racing, my heart pounding. My dad may have done some sketchy stuff in the past, but nothing like this. No, this is a whole new level of sketchiness for him.

"Hadley!" Londyn calls out from the side of the house. "Are you out here?"

I flip off the light and hold my breath as she shouts my name a few more times before giving up and going back inside. Then I quickly bury the bag, put the shovel away, and sneak back into the house. As I'm making a beeline for my room, I pass Payton on the stairway.

She stops when she notices the dirt on my hands. "Did you just go see what was in the bag Dad buried?"

I nod, wiping my hands off on the sides of my legs. "Yeah, it was just a bunch of alcohol bottles."

Her forehead creases. "Why would he bury that?"

I shrug, my insides jittery. "Probably because I told

him we weren't going to spend any more money on booze."

"He's such an asshole," Payton mutters then continues down the stairway.

"Yeah, he definitely is," I mutter in return then hurry up to my room.

"Hey, where were you just barely?" Londyn asks, setting down the book she was reading when I walk in. "I couldn't find you."

"Digging up a bag of alcohol Dad buried in the backyard." I flop down on my bed, avoiding eye contact with her.

"Seriously?" she asks, and I bob my head up and down. "Where the hell did he get all the money for it?"

I shrug, and then she starts to fume and rant. I listen to her, wishing I could tell her the truth, but I can't bring myself to do so. Not with this. No, whatever reason my dad has for burying drugs and money in the backyard can't be good, and I'd rather not have my sisters worry about it.

Still, I need to figure out why before he does something that gets us all hurt.

CHAPTER SIXTEEN

It takes me forever to fall asleep that night, and when I do, I sink into nightmares of the day my mom skidded off the road. The nightmare always plays out just like the memory of that day and always ends with that scream. I'm not even sure who the scream belonged to, yet the sound is branded into my mind like a hot iron searing flesh. I end up awakening before my alarm goes off with the sound of the scream echoing in my head.

Since the sun hasn't even risen yet, I try to go back to sleep, knowing I'm going to need my rest to deal with Blaise and his favors. Unfortunately, my mind's too wired and focused on that damn bag in the backyard.

Is my dad working for a drug dealer now? That'd

mean Blaise's dad is a drug dealer, which I guess could be possible.

There is another scenario, though. One that makes me restless with worry.

What if my dad stole the money and drugs from someone? Someone who's going to be awfully pissed off when they find out.

My stomach clenches in knots. What if the latter is true? What if my dad stole from, like, a drug lord or something? What if the drug lord comes after my sisters and me to get back at my dad?

"Fuck," I whisper, raking my fingers through my hair. "I need to chill out and stop overthinking this. Just find out the truth."

How am I supposed to do that? My dad sure as hell isn't going to tell me the truth. He hardly tells the truth anymore.

After half an hour of lying in bed, staring at the cracked ceiling, listening to Londyn snore, and stressing myself out, I give up on going back to sleep. I throw the blankets off, grab some clothes, and head to the bathroom to take a shower.

Since my family is fairly late risers, I figure everyone is still asleep, so when my dad steps out of his bedroom as I'm about to walk into the bathroom, I assume he's coming into the house from an all-night bender. Then I notice he's dressed in clean clothes, his face is freshly shaven, and his hair is combed. He's also digging around in his pocket for something.

"Are you just getting home or heading out somewhere?" I ask, grasping the bathroom doorknob.

He jolts, dropping whatever he dug out of his pocket. "Shit, you scared me." Exhaling a shaky breath, he scoops up the dropped object—a set of keys—then straightens and uses a key to lock up his bedroom door, fumbling a little like he's nervous. "You're up early."

"Yeah, so are you." I eyeball the deadbolt on his door that wasn't there when we moved in. "Did you just install that lock?"

He nods, stuffing the keys into his pocket. "Yeah, last night."

"Why?"

"Because I want some privacy."

"You say that like we snoop around in your room all the time."

His digs a pack of cigarettes out of the front pocket of his jacket, pops one into his mouth, and lights up. "Not all the time, but I know you guys do sometimes," he says through a cloud of smoke. "I've caught Payton going through my stuff a couple times. She needs to stop doing that. What's in my room is none of her damn business."

I raise a brow. "Like you haven't ever gone through our stuff?"

He takes another drag. "I'm the parent. I'm allowed to go through my daughters' stuff if I think I need to."

"The only reason you ever do is to steal money from us," I accuse, beyond irritated with him. Not just for what he's saying, but for locking the door.

First the bag in the backyard and now this? Just what is he up to?

Nothing good, I'm sure.

He ashes the cigarette onto the carpet with a hurt expression. "I've never stolen from you girls. I'm glad you think so lowly of me."

I almost feel bad. A couple days ago, I may have. Now I'm starting to get really tired of his crap.

"We used to not think that lowly of you," I admit. "But yeah, I'm not going to lie, lately, with the stuff you've been doing, my opinion of you has gone way down."

"Lately?" he questions. "All I've done lately is work to take care of you guys."

I resist an eye roll. Take care of us? He hasn't taken care of us since we lost our mom.

"You've had a steady job for a week, Dad, and God knows what the hell you're doing since you won't tell us where you work."

He shakily inhales from the end of his cigarette. "I work at the hardware store as a clerk."

Yeah right. I know he's lying. "If that's true, then why didn't you just tell me that last week when I asked?"

He lifts his shoulder, taking another drag. "Because you shouldn't be worrying about what I do … Sometimes I think you forget who the parent is."

"I understand you're my father, but as for a parent …" I suck in a breath. "Look, Dad, I'm eighteen now, and honestly, I've been taking care of myself and Londyn, Bailey, and Payton for years, so you may be our dad by blood, but as for the parent of this household, that's my job."

His lips part then shut. Then he shakes his head and storms toward the stairway. "I don't have time to argue with you, Hadley. I'm going to be late for work." He starts down the stairway, but then pauses and glances over his shoulder at me. "I'm going to be home late, but …" He scratches the back of his neck. "Do you guys want to meet me someplace for dinner?"

I stare at him, unsure if I heard him correctly. "You want us to go out to dinner with you?"

He nods, his arm falling to his side. "Yeah, I thought it might be nice to go out as a family. We haven't done that in a while, right?" He tries for a smile "It might be nice."

While the gesture is nice of him, we haven't had a family dinner with him in over eight years, and I really doubt any of my sisters are going to want to. Plus, with everything going on, I think it might be best to distance ourselves away from Dad.

He must read my hesitation all over my face, because he says, "Come on. Please say yes. I feel like I haven't talked to you girls in forever."

That's because he hasn't. Not about anything other than when our next move is.

"I won't take no for an answer," he adds, popping the end of his half-smoked cigarette into his mouth. "I'll text you the address of the place later, okay?" Then he hurries down the stairway before I can decline his offer.

Sighing heavily, I turn for the bathroom. Between dealing with Blaise this morning and my dad tonight, it's going to be a tough day.

SOMETIMES WHEN I'M HAVING A BAD DAY, I VISUALIZE myself graduating and being handed my diploma. Then I say goodbye to my sisters, hop into my car, and drive off to college without so much as a second glance back. Today, though, the images aren't bringing me as much comfort, and I think I know why.

Between the almost-skid-off-the-road incident yesterday and that bag being in the backyard, I'm not feeling the whole peace-out-old-life vibe. No, before I could ever leave, I'd have to make sure my dad hasn't … well, I'm not certain how to finish that sentence.

Needless to say, by the time I stroll up to Blaise's front door, I'm past being irritated and breezing right into don't-mess-with-me-because-I'm-pissed-off-at-my-shithead-father territory, something Blaise notices the second he opens the door.

"Wow, somebody doesn't look very happy to be here," he remarks, leaning against the doorframe with his arms folded.

Strangely, his stupid smirk isn't present. Not strange, he's dressed in black pants and a matching T-shirt. Seriously, it's like the Porterson brothers' trademark look.

"Can we please just cut the small talk and get straight to whatever the hell it is you want me to do?" I bite out bitterly.

He straightens, adjusting the leather bands covering his wrists. "Will you relax? I'm not going to have you do anything bad."

"I highly doubt that." I tuck a strand of hair behind my ear. "And besides, who said my bad mood has anything to do with you?"

A pucker forms between his brows. "You act like I'd be upset me if it wasn't about me."

"Don't pretend you don't get off on pissing me off."

He rubs his lips together, wrestling back a smile.

"Okay, maybe I do get off on it a little."

I roll my eyes. "Of course you do. I knew that from the moment I met you."

"That I'd get off on pissing you off?" His amusement magnifies.

"No, that you're the kind of guy who gets off on pissing girls off."

His smile dissolves. "That's not who I am at all."

"Liar." Sure, I may have discovered last night he didn't slash my tires or put up those flyers, but that doesn't erase the times he's purposely tried to grate under my skin. "You're totally the type of guy to get off on getting girls riled up. I can tell."

He shakes his head, strands of blond hair falling into his eyes. "Nope. I actually just do it with you."

My lip twitches in annoyance. "Why? Because I rejected you the first time we met? If so, that's really fucked up."

He gives a nonchalant shrug, his posture a bit stiff. "It wasn't just because of the rejection."

"Then, what else was it about?" I pry, curious if it has to do with why Alex loathes my family. If it has anything to do with my dad working for their dad.

All he does is offer me another shrug and, "You just bring that side out of me, I guess."

"So, you're putting the blame on me?"

"No. What I'm saying is that you do seem to get off

on pissing me off, too."

My mouth opens with a comeback, but then I zip my lips shut, realizing he's right. "Okay, maybe I do … a bit."

"Hmmm …" He rubs his jawline. "I wonder why that is." His tone carries insinuation. Why, who the hell knows?

I give a nonchalant shrug. "Probably because you're the most annoying person I've ever met."

"And you're the most stubborn girl I've ever met," he quips. Then he steps aside and motions for me to come in. "So, stubborn girl, quit stalling and come inside so you can complete your first favor."

I step over the threshold, arching my brow at him as I pass. "Please don't say you're going to start calling me stubborn girl now."

He bumps the door shut. "You wanted me to stop calling you sweetheart, didn't you?"

I waver my head from side to side. "Yeah, I guess so."

He smiles as he lightly tugs on a stand of my hair. "So, stubborn girl it is." Then he takes off toward a hallway. "I'll be right back. I just have to grab my stuff."

Before I can ask what he's grabbing, he disappears down the hallway.

I'm left standing alone in his living room, which is surprisingly clean. The furniture is decent, too, way better than anything my family owns. The Portersons also have a flat screen television, an item my family hasn't owned in a while, ever since my dad took ours and pawned it. He tried to lie about it when I confronted him, but I found the receipt in his pocket while I was doing the laundry. He never would admit what he did with the extra cash, which I guess is kind of his MO. Well, that and getting drunk.

Talk about a great father figure.

Sighing audibly, I trudge over to the sofa to sit down when Rhyland comes wandering into the room, carrying a bowl of cereal. His hair is damp, as if he just got out of the shower, and he's wearing black jeans and a blue T-shirt.

Huh. So they do own different colored clothing.

He pauses mid-bite when his gaze lands on me. "Hey." He lowers the spoon from his mouth and wipes a dribble off milk off his chin with the back of his hand. "You're here early."

"Because I was ordered to be." My tone comes out light instead of bitter, like I was aiming for.

Man, I really must be tired.

He smiles, relaxing as he plops down on the leather sofa and kicks his feet up onto the table. "Glad to see you're being chill about the bet." He stuffs another bite of cereal into his mouth then pats the cushion, indicating for me to sit down. "Alex thought you'd bail out of this whole favors thing."

Rolling my eyes, I take a seat. "Of course he did."

"I didn't, though," Rhyland clarifies with an easy smile.

I twist to face him, bringing my knee up onto the cushion between us. "Oh yeah? And why's that?"

He raises a shoulder. "You don't seem like the type to back down. Yesterday proves that."

"True." I can't tell if he's insulting me or not.

"That's a good thing," he assures me, as if reading my mind. "At least, I think so." He rotates, facing me. "I have to say, after watching you race, I definitely think you should start racing on weekends."

"Why?" I question. "I didn't even win against your brother."

"Yeah, but you've got mad skills. Seriously, a lot of people would've overcorrected when they hit that patch of gravel, but you handled it like a fucking boss."

I shrug, my stomach getting queasy at the reminder of how I almost walked in my mom's footsteps yesterday. "I've had a lot of practice."

"With almost skidding road?" he teases with a smile.

I roll my tongue in my mouth, trying not to smile back. "No, with racing."

His phone buzzes from inside his pocket, and he digs it out. "How long have you been doing it?" he asks, frowning at something on the screen.

I wonder what's on his phone that's got him looking all Charlie Brown.

"Since I got my driver's license. But I started going to drag races when I was, like, four." There I go again. Talking about my life aloud to a Porterson. Have I not learned my lesson?

His gaze elevates to mine in surprise. "Since you were four? Holy shit, that's young."

A slow breath eases from my lips. "My mom was into it and wanted me to be into it, too. Guess it worked."

"She *was*?" he asks with a hint of pity.

My chest tightens a bit. "She died a while ago."

"I'm so sorry." His Adam's apple bobs up and down as he swallows hard. "That's got to be hard. To lose your parent at such a young age, I mean. Blaise and Jaxon's mom died when they were both young. My mom actually raised them. Well, until Blaise was old enough to get guardianship of us. That was one of the best day of our lives."

Wow. No wonder I couldn't find anything online about Blaise's mom. I feel bad for him and Jaxon, and kind of for Rhyland and Alex, too. If their eighteen-year-old brother got guardianship of them, things with their mom had to be super effed up.

"What was the best day of your life?" Blaise asks as he re-enters the room, his gaze dancing back and forth between Rhyland and me, and his lips sinking into a frown.

"The day you became my dad." Rhyland grins as he rises to his feet.

Blaise rolls his eyes. "How many times have I told you guys not to call me that? You're almost as old as me."

"Which is why we do it." Rhyland walks up to Blaise and whispers something quietly enough that I can't hear.

Blaise grimaces, grinding his teeth from side to side. "Fine, I'll handle it."

"Sorry, man. I'd do it myself, but you know he won't be as cooperative if I go." Rhyland pats Blaise on the shoulder then smiles genuinely at me. "Thanks for talking to me this morning, Hadley. We should make it our morning routine for the next month."

"Am I going to have to come over here every morning?" I direct my question to Blaise.

"Maybe," he replies distractedly, fumbling to get his keys out of his pocket. Then he turns for the door, nodding for me to follow.

As I trudge after him, Rhyland whispers to me, "Go easy on him this morning, okay? He's really stressed out about some stuff and is having a rough morning." He doesn't wait for me to nod, just waves and takes off down the hallway.

"You coming?" Blaise asks grumpily from the doorway

My initial instinct is to fire a snarky remark at him, but Rhyland's words replay in my head, so I end up just nodding. Call me a softy, but I have a tender spot for people who are stressed out, especially eighteen-year-olds who have guardianship over their younger brothers, and maybe his sister, too.

While mine and Blaise's stories aren't exactly the same, they're pretty close. What I wonder, though, is: how did he get guardianship of his siblings? Not just in the sense of legal terms, but what led him to the point where things were so bad that he decided he needed to become a parent at eighteen? It's kind of remarkable when I really think about it, and tragically sad at the same time. That he had to do something so selfless—giving up his future for his siblings. And as much as I've despised Blaise over the last week or so, I question if he's a better person than me in some ways.

Because, while I may ponder the idea of getting guardianship of my sisters, I've never actually looked into it, even with how bad my dad is getting. Instead, I've been daydreaming of taking off. Of making *my* life better.

Does that make me a bad person? A selfish one?

I'm not sure, but the thought makes a heavy amount of guilt weigh down on my shoulders.

CHAPTER SEVENTEEN

BLAISE AND I SPEND THE NEXT TEN MINUTES SILENTLY driving toward town in his SUV. He doesn't even turn the radio on to fill the silence. I'm left wanting to bang my head against the window. Seriously, I'm getting so desperate I'm even starting to miss arguing with him. Plus, he hasn't told me where we're going.

About fifteen minutes into the drive, Blaise receives a text. After reading the message, he mutters, "Fuck, he's worse than I thought." Then he drops his phone into the cupholder and grows quiet again.

Finally, I can't take the maddening silence and uncertainty anymore.

"So, are you going to tell me where we're going and what I'll be doing for you?"

His jaw is set tight as he focuses on the road. "I'm still deciding what part I'm going to have you play in this. As for where we're going, it's to a house Alex is at."

Okay, evasive much?

"And why are we going there?" I check the time on the dashboard clock. "And how long is this going to take? I'm supposed to drive my sisters to school this morning."

"Shit, I didn't even think about that." He rakes his fingers through his hair then gives me a sidelong glance. "Can Londyn maybe drive them? This might take a bit."

"How long is a bit? Because school starts in less than an hour."

He rubs his lips together. "Yeah, you might be a little late."

"Being late to school wasn't part of the deal," I stress. "And I can't be late. Not after being tardy to all my morning classes yesterday, and then skipping out on the last half of the day."

He looks at me with one hand resting on the wheel. "Yeah, I noticed you weren't in last period. What was that about?"

"We have last period together?" I ask, and he nods. I'm not sure whether to frown or not. I don't know how I feel about him after what I heard last night and with what Rhyland just told me.

Conflicted. That's what I am. Conflicted because he sometimes seems like a nice guy, yet seems like an asshole other times.

The edges of his lips kick up into a smile, but his eyes remain clouded with worry. "Aw, come on. You don't need to look so sad about it. I promise not to bug you too much. Or, well, at least I'll try not to."

"I'm not sad," I reply with a shrug. "I'm undecided."

His brow meticulously arches. "About what exactly?"

"About having you in my classes."

"Hmmm … Interesting."

"No, not really."

He assesses me closely. "Actually, it sort of is."

I refuse to squirm under his unwavering gaze. "And why's that?"

He shrugs, refocusing on the road. "Because, if you're undecided about me being in another one of your classes, it means you're undecided about me."

"And that's a good thing because …?"

He shrugs. "I don't know."

"Okay …" God, this is the most evasive conversation ever.

We grow silent again as Blaise stares at the road, drumming his fingers on top of the steering wheel. Since it clearly seems like he doesn't want to talk or give me any sort of confirmation about how long we're going to be or what we're even doing, I dig out my phone and send Londyn a text.

Me: Hey, so I'm gonna need you to drive everyone to school today.

Londyn: What!? Why?

Me: Because my first favor is going to probably take too long for me to get back in time.

Londyn: That's so not cool. You need to make sure Blaise understands that you can't be late for school.

Me: Yeah, I'll try.

Londyn: Don't try. Do.

Me: All right, boss.

Londyn: Sorry. I'm not trying to be bossy, but we can't let these guys walk all over us.

Me: Hey! Think about who you're talking to. You know there's no way I'll let that happen. Blaise just didn't inform me until we were way across town that this favor is going to take a while. But I made it clear being late for school is so not cool with me.

Londyn: Good. You may be in some stupid, twisted bet with him, but that doesn't mean he gets to mess up school for you. And what are you even doing for him?

Me: Not sure yet, but I think it has something to do with Alex.

Londyn: You need to be careful then. He's the worst. I know he's the one who put those flyers up.

Me: Yeah, me, too.

I want to tell her about the conversation I overheard last night between Alex and Blaise, but I don't want to think about it myself.

We text for a bit longer until she finally agrees to drive everyone, and by the time I pocket my phone, Blaise is driving past the last of the houses lining the main road and steering out onto the highway.

"We're really far out here," I comment, glancing at the trees and desolate farmland bordering the road.

Shit, should I be worried? I mean, I'm a girl in a car alone with a guy who has a questionable police record. Sure, I know some self-defense, but that doesn't mean I want to put myself in a situation where I'd have to try to use my skills.

"I'm sorry. This is probably really weird. I know that." Blaise slows down and flips on the blinker. "I promise nothing bad's going to happen. Or, well, at least not to you. Alex, on the other hand, is about to get into some deep shit." He turns down a dirt road that winds into the hills.

"Why?" I ask, gripping the handle above me as the road becomes bumpy. "What'd he do?"

He grips the wheel tighter as we hit another bump. "Nothing he hasn't done before, which is why I'm so pissed off. He never fucking learns his lessons." He blows out a deafening breath, his gaze sliding to mine.

"Look, for my first favor, can you just not tell anyone what you're about to witness?"

My nerves rise a notch. "Um, yeah … just as long as it's not like a hardcore crime where someone's hurting someone, then yeah, I can do that."

"The only person getting hurt is Alex, and he's doing it to himself," he replies tightly, his knuckles whitening on the wheel.

I should feel better. Not telling anyone about this seems like an easy enough favor. And I shouldn't care that Alex is hurting himself—the guy is a jerk. But the look in Blaise's eyes … the self-tormenting guilt over something he can't control … yeah, I've been there. With my sisters. With my father. Even with myself sometimes.

I swallow down the pain creeping up on me the best I can as Blaise parks in front of a singlewide trailer at the end of the bumpy road. The siding is peeling off, all the windows are boarded up, and half the roof is covered up with a tarp. The landscaping isn't any better-looking either; the grass yellowing and covered in old car parts and tires. I've lived in my fair share of dumpy places and areas, but this house gives all those a run for their money. I mean, at least the homes we lived in had roofs.

"So, whose place is this?" I wonder as Blaise silences the engine.

He makes no move to get out, resting his arms on top of the steering wheel as he stares at the trailer. "It's an … acquaintance of my father's."

"Oh." His infamous father, the criminal who my dad might be working for. *Lovely.*

Blaise's gaze skates to me. "From your tone, I'm guessing you've heard about my dad."

"Well, I did read all that stuff about your family. The internet seems to have a lot to say about him," I reply nonchalantly.

"Yeah, I forgot you did that." He studies me with mild curiosity. "How did you do that anyway? Break into those records?"

I tap my finger against my lips. "Now, why would I tell you my secrets?"

"Come on," he pleads. "In fact, it can be my favor for this morning."

I shake my head, *tsking* him. "Now, Blaise, you only get one a day, and you already used that one."

"No one said I only get one a day." When I still refuse to tell him, he sighs. "Fine, I'll just ask you again tomorrow."

"That's really how you want to waste your favors?" I ask, digging my sunglasses out of my purse.

He shrugs, nibbling on his bottom lip as he surveys the trailer. "Seems like as good of a favor as any."

"You know, you could always just ask Alex. I mean,

I'm sure he can tell you all about my family's secrets since he gathered all that info for the flyers."

Wait. Why am I telling him this?

Dammit, I really should've grabbed some coffee before I left the house. I'm too tired.

Question marks flood his eyes. "You say that like I didn't have any part of it, which I did."

Liar. But his protective nature toward his brother is something I can respect, so I decide not to tell him I know the truth.

I pick at my fingernails. "Okay, then maybe you already know the answer."

He examines me suspiciously. "What do you know?"

"I know a lot of things," I assure him with a sugary sweet smile. "I'm super clever. But I'm sure you've already caught on to that. Well, if you're clever, too."

"No, you know something about my family," he accuses. "I can tell."

"Would it matter if I did? I mean, yesterday Alex said it didn't matter if I told the entire school about your family's dirty laundry. That people already know everything about your family, and that they respect you too much to do anything. So, what would babbling a dirty little secret about you guys matter?"

"That's nowhere near the truth," he grumbles. "Alex just likes to run his mouth, which usually gets him in trouble."

"Trouble like this?" I nod at the house.

"No, this is trouble he does to himself."

I think I'm starting to get the gist of what's going on inside that trailer, why Blaise had to drive out here. I'm not that surprised. I've wondered a few times if Alex was strung out.

"What's he on?" I dare ask.

"What's he not on?" He sinks back into the seat and looks me straight in the eye. "Look, Hadley, you have to swear to me that you won't tell anyone about this. I know Alex and I have treated you like shit, but I really need you to do me a solid right now and let what's about to happen stay between you, me, and Alex, okay? I don't even want Rhyland to know."

"Rhyland doesn't already know?"

"Well, he sort of does, but he doesn't realize how bad Alex is getting. And honestly, I wouldn't have even brought you out here if I'd known how bad he is going to be … When Rhyland first told me I needed to pick Alex up, I thought he was just hungover. But then Alex messaged me while I was driving up here and … I can tell he's messed up pretty bad." His gaze slides to me again, a silent plea filling his eyes. "Can you please just promise me you won't say anything to anyone about this? Not even your sisters. Alex … he's been in a lot of trouble, which I'm sure you already know, and if the wrong people find out what he's messed up in ..." He gulps. "Just promise me, okay?"

I wonder what he means by wrong people. The police? Yeah, I have a feeling there's more to it than that. I could ask him, but with how hush-hush he's acting right now, I doubt he'll tell me.

"I said I wouldn't tell anyone, and I meant it," I assure him. "I may think your brother is an asshole, but I totally understand the whole protective sibling thing. Plus, my dad's an alcoholic and drug addict, so I have a good idea of how this is going to go down."

His brows furrow as he stares at me. "You're different from what I first thought."

"Okay ...? Is that a good or bad thing?" Not that I care. I'm just curious.

"It's an ... undecided thing."

"Touché, dude."

That makes him chuckle, but only for a brief moment. Then he goes right back into worrying mode, a place I constantly reside.

Stillness surrounds us, and the longer her remains sitting in the car, the more I wonder what he's waiting for.

"Are you going to go in there and get him?" I finally ask. "Or is he supposed to come out here?"

He checks his phone and frowns. "I'm sure I'm going

to have to go in and drag his high-ass out. I'm just giving myself a moment to mentally prepare myself."

"For having to deal with him?" That I can understand. I have to do it with my dad all the time.

"For that and for dealing with the other people inside."

"You mean, your father's acquaintances?"

He nods, stuffing his phone into his pocket. "They're complicated to deal with."

I rest back in the seat and tuck my legs underneath me. "Why?"

His brow curves upward as he glances at me. "You ask a lot of questions."

"Not normally, but yeah, when someone drives me out to the middle of nowhere to what I'm guessing is a crack house, I start to get a little question-y."

"It's not a crack house," he swears. "My dad actually owns the home and the land. He lets the people who work for him live here. He owns quite a few houses in Honeyton. All of them equally as shitty as this one, except his own."

"Does he own your house?"

"No, my mom does ... or, well, she did until ..." He hastily clears his throat. "But yeah, once I turned eighteen, I became the official owner of the shithole that is my home."

"That's pretty cool that you own the place."

"I guess." He shrugs, sadness creeping into his expression. "Sometimes I wish I was living in some shitty apartment in some big-ass city, paying way too much for rent and spending my days doing … well, anything but this." He clears his throat again then shoves open the door. "But yeah, anyway, I'm going to go drag Alex out. Be back in a minute … hopefully." He jumps out and slams the door. Then I watch him hike across the grass to the front door. He knocks once then walks inside and closes the door behind him.

As I sit in the quietness of the SUV, waiting for him to come back out, I replay everything Blaise just said. Some of the stuff was, I think, accidental, like the part about wishing he lived somewhere else. I don't know why he confided in me, even accidentally. Maybe because he's overly stressed out? I can understand that. I've babbled crap I wanted to retract when my mind was overworked. Hell, I've done it while I was talking to Blaise and to Rhyland.

All questions aside, I think I learned something else this morning. That my initial impression of Blaise was incorrect. He may not be as big of a jerk as I originally assumed. Perhaps he was really just trying to protect his brother. Although, there were a few times I can't blame his asshatery on Alex. Like the first time we met. Or the time he saved me from getting detention and thought I owed him. Or, and quite possibly the biggest, when he threw that kiss into the deal. Of course the kiss itself wasn't awful. I'm never going to admit that aloud.

"Just exactly who are you, Blaise Porterson?" I mumble to myself as I stare at the house. "The cocky jerk I first met? Or the guy who's in that house, taking care of his brother?"

The longer I analyze the questions, the more I become highly aware of something else. Something that makes me very uncomfortable.

I'm obsessing over a guy and breaking my own rules. How the hell did this happen? It's not like I want to date Blaise, but I am thinking about him way too much.

"Get your shit together, Hadley," I tell myself in a firm tone. "Stop worrying about Blaise and just focus on getting through this deal so you can go on with your life and your plans."

To busy myself, I retrieve my phone and message Londyn.

Me: Everything go good this morning?

Londyn: Yep. We're all good. Even Payton didn't put up too much of a fuss about going. After yesterday, I thought she might, but she seemed okay. The only weird thing is that I tried to go into Dad's room

to grab the spare key to your car because I lost mine, and his door was locked.

Me: Yeah, I know. I caught him locking it up this morning. He seemed really sketchy about it, too, but that's Dad for you. And FYI, Dad doesn't have a spare key to my car anymore. I took it away that time he took my car and didn't return it for three days.

Londyn: Oh! I'm so glad you did, but I wish you'd told me. Could have saved me some time this morning.

Me: Yeah, sorry about that. I put the spare key under my mattress. Are you guys still at the house? Because it's late.

Londyn: No, we made it to school.

Me: Oh, did you find your key then?

Londyn: Not exactly.

Me: Okay ... Did you get a ride with Dad then?

Londyn: Ha, what a funny joke.

I chuckle, yet I'm still confused.

Me: How did you get to school then? Did you walk?

Londyn: Well, we were going to, even though it was really late, but ... Look, promise me you won't get mad, because we did get to school on time and nothing bad happened.

I rest back in the seat and prop my feet onto the dash as I type.

Me: I'm not going to get mad. You're responsible. I trust your judgment.

Londyn: But I may have screwed up a bit with this one, but only because I panicked about us all being late to school. I tried to call Hunter for a ride, because he's like the only person I know in this town, but he didn't answer, so I decided we were going to walk and just be late. But on our way out, someone else we sort of know saw us and asked if we needed a ride. At first, I declined because this person is a straight-up jerk. Or, well, he seemed that way at first, but then I realized we were going to be super late, and Bailey and Payton were complaining, and I panicked, and ... I'm so sorry!

Me: Sorry for what? For accepting a ride? You're acting really weird.

Londyn: Not just for accepting a ride. For accepting a ride from our neighbors.

Me: Wait. You got a ride with the Portersons?

Londyn: Yeah, Rhyland and Jaxon anyway. I'm sorry. I love you, and I'm still unsure about them. I just become a terrible decision-maker when I'm desperate. I'm so, so sorry. I feel like I stabbed you in the back. Please don't hate me.

Me: Why would I hate you? You needed to find a ride to school, so you found one. And Rhyland and

Jaxon don't seem too terrible, I guess. Well, Rhyland doesn't. Jaxon's too quiet to tell for sure.

Londyn: I know, but still ... I said all those bad things about them and told everyone we should stay away from them. I'm a complete hypocrite. And you made that bet so they'd leave us alone, and then we ended up being around them anyway.

Me: The bet wasn't a waste. It gives us assurance that shit like the flyer incident won't happen again. And besides, Alex was the main culprit behind that. And the tires. Not Rhyland or Jaxon.

Londyn: I know, but I still feel awful.

Me: Well, don't. Part of being in charge is putting others' needs before yours. You needed a ride, so you got a ride, and no one was late. You did good, sis.

Londyn: If you say so, but I still feel a bit like a traitor. At least tell me you're doing okay. That Blaise hasn't been too awful.

Me: I'm fine. And Blaise is okay, I guess. At least he's been less cocky this morning.

Londyn: That's good. Did you have to do the favor yet?

I hesitate. While I lie to my sisters a lot, it's mostly to protect them. If I don't tell her the truth now, though, it's to protect Blaise and Alex. But I made a promise to Blaise, and since I understand that protective need toward my siblings, the idea of confessing his secret doesn't feel right.

Me: Nah, not yet. But I think he's probably just going to make me run in and get them coffee after we pick up Alex.

Londyn: Great, so he's playing the servant card?

Me: I think so.

Londyn: I want to say I'm surprised, but I'm not. He's such a jerk.

I should correct her, tell her that maybe he isn't as horrible as we thought, but that would lead to a bunch of other questions that I'll have to lie about. And since my tally for the day is going up really quickly, I decide to just let it drop.

Londyn: Crap, I have to go. Class is about to start. But you're going to be here soon, right?

Me: Yeah, I'll be there in a bit.

I hope.

After I finish texting Londyn, I sit in the SUV for another handful of minutes before I start to get really bored. And hot. Blaise left the windows rolled up and took the keys with him, and with the sun being fully risen, even though I wore a pair of shorts and a black T-shirt, the cab is starting to heat up fast. The more time that ticks by, the more my skin dampens with sweat.

I'd text Blaise, except I don't have his number. I don't have any of the Portersons' digits.

About an hour in, I start to lose my cool. Not only is it stifling hot, but I'm miles away from town and it's getting late.

"Fuck this shit." I climb out of the car and stare down the driveway, trying to mentally calculate the distance back to town. It has to be at least a dozen miles.

I could always hotwire Blaise's SUV, but I wouldn't put it past him or Alex to call the cops on my thieving ass. Blaise never said I couldn't go into the house, but it was sort of implied when he got out and didn't invite me in. Then again, if he didn't want me to go in, he shouldn't have left me in the car for over an hour.

Squaring my shoulders, I march up to the house. Yeah, the place is beyond creep, and I'm not so sure I'm buying into it not being a crack house, but I've been to places like this before. A lot of times actually, needing to pick up my dad or settle a deal with someone my dad tried to screw over.

Payton also went through a phase about six months ago when she was spending a lot of time with a guy who was really into drugs. She swore to me she didn't do any drugs with him, but that didn't mean I just willingly let her hang out with him. No, she'd sneak off, and I'd have to drive to the dude's house and drag her ass out kicking and screaming. He lived in a really sketchy area.

While I hate to judge this house by its torn-up side and lack of a roof, Blaise's hesitation to go inside is enough for me to know that what's on the inside isn't going to be a welcome mat and a place smelling of freshly baked cookies.

But I got this.

I always got this.

CHAPTER EIGHTEEN

WHEN I ARRIVE AT THE FRONT DOOR, I MUSTER UP A DEEP breath, collect my shit, and knock.

"Who the fuck is that?" a voice snaps from the other side. "We weren't expecting anyone else, were we?"

I wince, but I keep my feet planted to the ground.

"I sure as hell wasn't," someone yells back.

They grow quiet.

I knock again, harder this time.

"Fuck." Someone lets out a string of curses, then the door is cracked open. A trail of smoke snakes outside as a guy peers out at me, his gaze sweeping up and down me. "Who the hell are you?"

"I'm a …" I almost say a friend of Blaise's, but that doesn't seem accurate. "Look, I drove up here with Blaise, and I really need to talk to him."

The guy's bloodshot eyes measure me up. "Why?"

"Because …" I shift my weight, feeling more uneasy than I'd like. "Can you just tell him to come here please? It's an emergency."

He gives a lengthy, very annoying pause, then steps back and opens the door. "I've got a better idea, sweetheart. How about you come inside and get him yourself?"

Every one of my muscles twitch at his use of *sweetheart*, but now that I have a very good view of this guy, I decide to bite my tongue, unlike when Blaise called me the same stupid pet name. Unlike Blaise, this guy isn't a cocky teenager who's annoyingly pretty. No, he's a grown-ass pain with scabs on his face, track marks on his arms, and a pipe in his hand.

"Well, well, well, what do we have here?" someone else asks.

I turn and find another man lounging on a leather recliner that's perched in the center of a small room made of chipped, wooden walls and shaggy, orange carpet. Where the man in front of me is obviously drugged out, this guy looks like a steroid freak, all bulging muscles and acne.

"I'm not sure yet." The guy in front of me fixes his gaze on me. "What's your name?" When I make no move to offer my name, he adds, "If you don't tell me who you are, sweetheart, then I can't show you where Blaise is."

My fingers curl inward. God, what I'd give to crack my knuckles against this jerk's scabby face.

"It's Belinda," I lie.

"Belinda?" He doesn't seem too impressed. Either that or he doesn't believe me. "So, why are you here, Belinda?"

"I already told you this." Irritation surfaces in my tone, despite my internal battle not to go all smartass on this guy. "I need to talk to Blaise."

"Hmm …" He rubs his jawline, causing a scab to fall off. I nearly gag. "I'm not sure if there's a Blaise here." He trades a look with the other guy. "What do you think, D? Is there a Blaise here?"

The dude on the sofa—D—eyes me over, a smile curling at his lips. "Actually, my name's Blaise."

"I'm sure it is," I say snidely. "That's why he just called you D."

"D's my middle name," D insists as he rises to his feet and crosses the room toward me. "So, what did you want to talk to me about? Or should we go somewhere more private?"

"Just tell me where Blaise is." I give him a blank stare, pretending to be the epitome of indifference. Deep down, though, uneasiness stirs. This situation is bad, especially since I can't see Blaise anywhere. But he has to be here. I saw him go in, and he never left … unless there's a back door.

Crap, what if there's a back door? What if he left me? But, where would he go? And why would he just leave his car here? Those questions should relieve me, but there have been plenty of times when my dad ditched me and left his truck behind. He even took his truck keys with him so I couldn't drive away, which is the main reason I taught myself how to hotwire a car.

"I already told you, baby, I'm right here." Steroid freak gives me a grin that sends a chill down my spine. Then he reaches for me, to do who knows what. I never get to find out, because I grab his wrist and twist his arm.

"Fuck!" he howls in pain. "Let go of me, you bitch."

"Not until you tell me where Blaise is," I threaten, twisting his arm harder.

Scab face starts to lunge for me, and I lift my leg, preparing to kick him in the balls. He notices before I make contact and swings around, coming at me from the side while steroid freak reaches for something in his pocket.

My pulse quickens. Crap, this is getting out of hand fast.

"Hadley …? What the hell?" Blaise appears in the doorway of the living room.

I breathe in relief, so thankful to see him, which is a bit strange, but justifiable.

"Hey," I say, sounding all casual, though I'm one twist away from breaking steroid freak's arm.

Blaise tilts his head curiously as he assesses the scene. "What're you doing?"

"Oh, you know, just getting acquainted with your friends." I release steroid freak's arm and step back as he whirls toward me. "I don't think they like me."

Steroid freak glares at me, gripping his arm. "You're going to pay for that," he growls, stepping toward me.

"Touch her and I'll break your fingers," Blaise warns. "And I'll make sure my father knows how shitty you treated Mel's daughter."

Steroid freak slams to a screeching halt. "You're Mel's daughter?" Nervousness edges into his features.

"Yeah …?" I glance at Blaise for help. "How does this dude know my dad?"

"Because he works for—"

"D, don't you and El have some shit to do?" Blaise cuts steroid freak off, crossing the room toward us.

"Wait. Your names are El and D?" My gaze flicks between the two guys standing near me, and I snicker. "Let me guess. You shortened your real names so you could remember them. Or did you just forget them altogether and picked a letter from the alphabet?"

D glowers at me, but with a quick, stern look from

Blaise, he looks away to El. "Let's get out of here. We've got a lot of shit to get done, and I'm over dealing with girl drama."

"Yeah, like I'm the one who started it," I mutter as El and D move for the door.

D throws me a dirty look before walking out, and El follows, slamming the door.

Blaise immediately gapes at me. "Seriously, how has that mouth of yours never gotten you in trouble before?"

"Who says it hasn't?" When he shakes his head unfathomably, I shrug. "You should already know I speak my mind. It's what made you hate me right from the start."

"I didn't and still don't hate you," he insists, stuffing his hands into the back pockets of his jeans. "You just … I don't know, threw me off a bit. You're very …" He considers something carefully. "Well, I think Alex said it best when he said you're feisty."

"I'm not feisty," I deny. "I just don't like to put up with guy drama."

"Guy drama?" His brow cocks. "All I did was call you sweetheart, and you told me to go fuck myself and then some."

"Just because I'm a girl doesn't mean I like to be called vomit-inducing pet names," I scoff. "Guys need to realize that."

"No one's ever complained about me doing it before," Blaise points out. "In fact, most girls like it when I call them, as you put it, vomit-inducing pet names."

"Yeah, well, I'm a special kind of girl then, I guess. But I know I'm not one of a kind. You should consider that the next time you start throwing around gross pet names to complete strangers."

He silently stares at me, either irritated or utterly thrown off—I can't tell. "I'll make sure to do that." He pauses. "But I definitely disagree with you not being one of a kind. You're very odd."

"Gee, thanks … I think."

"It's not a bad thing," he quickly says. "Just different."

"I wouldn't care if it was bad or not," I tell him confidently. "I've been called a hell of a lot worse than odd."

"Yeah, I'm not that surprised."

When I attempt to glare at him, although my lips become traitorous bastards and threaten to turn upward, he chuckles and shakes his head.

"Hadley, you almost just broke a drug dealer's arm, and I'm guessing that probably isn't the first time you've done something like that. That's not normal."

"Hey, I've never tried to break a drug dealer's arm before," I deny indignantly. As his brows elevate in doubt, I heave a dramatic sigh. "Okay, it may have happened one other time. But in my defense, both times the guys deserved it. The first dude screwed around with my sister and cheated on her. And that D guy"—I aim a finger at the door—"was reaching for me first before I grabbed his arm. It was total self-defense."

"I believe you. D can be a real prick, which is part of the reason I didn't have you come in here with me to begin with."

I raise my hands in front of me. "Look, dude, you left me in the car with the windows up for over an hour, and we're in the middle of nowhere; what else was I supposed to do? It's not like I could've texted you. I don't even have your number."

He bites back a smile. "Is that your way of asking for my number?"

"What? No." I pull a repulsed face. "That's the last thing I want."

"Sure it is." His cockiness returns in full form, smirk and all. It makes me want to smack that smugness right of his pretty boy face.

Instead, I settle for poking him in the chest. "Didn't I just tell you not to assume I want certain things?"

His smirk doubles. "It's not an assumption if you just said you wanted it."

"Good God, you're so annoying," I growl out. Then I raise my chin and turn for the door. "You know what?

I'm out of here. I've done my favor for the day. I don't need to deal with this crap."

He snags the bottom of my shirt before I make it too far. "I'm not going to just let you walk home. We're in the middle of nowhere."

I rotate around and try to pry his fingers from the back of my shirt. "Let me? You can't make me do anything."

He refuses to let go. "I know, but … we have a deal. You owe me a favor."

"You said my silence was today's favor," I grit through my teeth, resorting to tugging on my shirt.

"Yeah, well, I want two favors this morning." He holds my shirt tighter.

"No way. I'm not just going to give you an extra favor." Deep down, I don't really want to walk home. But the fact that he thinks he can tell me not to is infuriating.

"Will you just quit arguing? You're just being difficult to be difficult."

"No, I'm not."

"Yes you are." He heaves an exasperated breath when I tug on my shirt again. "Will you please just listen to me for a minute? I'm not trying to be controlling. I'm trying to help you."

"Sure you are." I yank on my shirt again, refusing to listen. Sure, we may have had a small moment of understanding in the car, but that doesn't mean I'm going to let him boss me around now.

When I pull on my shirt again, I throw my weight into it and end up losing my balance. I trip backward, my fingers falling from my shirt as I reach out to grip his arm for support. But he stumbles over his own feet and we both end up falling.

I wince as my back hits the floor and Blaise lands on top of me, his chest pressing against mine. He does manage to get his hands down at the very last second, softening some of the impact, but his knees bang against my shins.

He hurriedly pushes back, staring down at me worriedly. "Holy shit, are you okay?"

I bob my head up and down, blinking as my eyes water from the pain in my shins. "Yeah, I think so. Just as long as you'll get off me." I lightly shove his chest.

He slightly lifts his weight off me. "I will, but only if you promise not to walk home. This part of town … it's not always safe."

"I'm not going to let you scare me into staying here." I push on his chest again, but he doesn't budge. "Dude, don't make me put you in a headlock."

He chuckles, his eyes crinkling around the corners. "I'm not so sure that's a threat."

I lift a brow. "Are you questioning my headlock ability?"

"No, not at all." His expression is completely serious. "It just wouldn't bother me as much as you'd want it to."

"You say that now, but twenty bucks says you tap out within the first minute."

He laughs wholeheartedly this time, and the sight makes him look ridiculously pretty. It's both irritating and mesmerizing.

"This isn't funny." I pinch his nipple.

"You're seriously violent." He pushes back to rub his chest, laughter still tickling his tone until he sighs. "Look, I don't want to fight with you, or be the guy pinning you down to the floor—well, for this reason anyway—but I'm trying to protect you. I swear." His loud exhale sweeps across my face, his breath minty. "There's a lot about this town you don't know about yet. And there're some areas … and certain people who are … trouble. Trust me; you don't want to go wandering around alone out here."

He's being too evasive. I need more of an explanation.

"Does this have anything to do with my dad working for your dad?"

He wavers, studying me. "So, you know about that?"

"Well, you did just mention my dad to those guys who work for your dad. I can put two and two together." I'm not ready to divulge that I overheard him talking to Alex.

"Shit, I forgot I said that." He lowers his head as he curses under his breath. He's so close now that his hair is tickling my cheek. It feels weirdly nice, having him this close. And for some stupid reason, it makes me think of that kiss yesterday. That kiss that felt like it burned me up from the inside out.

Deep down, inside a part I'll never admit exists, I want to press my lips to his, which is why I lean away from him.

"Was I not supposed to know my dad works for yours?" I tilt my head to the other side.

Sighing, he meets my gaze. "Sort of. I mean, your dad asked us not to say anything. Said you wouldn't understand."

"How considerate of him," I reply dryly. "And I'm sure there's more to it than that. There always is with my dad." When he shifts his weight, seeming awfully squirmy, I ask, "Is there something you're not telling me?"

He shrugs awkwardly as he props himself up on one arm. "If there is, it's not like I'd tell you."

"Well, that's rude."

"Well, isn't the whole point of not telling someone just that? To not tell them, even if it's rude? Besides, didn't you just give me a whole speech while we were in the car about you knowing things you weren't telling me and that you weren't obligated to tell me, even if I asked?"

"It wasn't a speech," I correct. "It was a simple statement."

He presses back a grin. "I'm starting to realize that, with you, nothing is simple … You're a very intense girl."

"You're the one who's lying on top of me. I think, right now, that statement might describe you more than it does me."

"Yeah, but I'm not a girl," he points out amusedly.

"Huh, could've fooled me." In a sick, twisted way, I'm kind of enjoying getting under his skin, which shit, is something he already accused me of.

I have no idea what's wrong with me. I'm not usually this persistent with tormenting guys or anyone in general. Then again, people usually give up more easily. Blaise is as stubborn as me.

He mockingly scowls at me. "Hey, I'm not girlie-looking."

"You're pretty, though." I shrug. "Pretty is a girlie word."

He shakes his head, gaping at me. "I'm not pretty. I have piercings and tattoos, and the way I dress … none of that is girlie."

I struggle not to smile, totally getting off on this. *I'm screwed up. I really am. What the hell is wrong with me?*

"Girlie girls can have piercings and tattoos, so I don't think that saves your ass. Besides, even if it did, I don't see any of these alleged piercings and tattoos."

His brow curves upward. "You don't believe I have them?"

"No, I don't." I grin at the look on his face. "It's amusing how irritated you are about that."

"Yeah, well, you're about to be equally as irritated." He sticks out his tongue that, sure enough, is glinting with a metallic piercing. "See? Piercing." Then he dips his head and licks the side of my neck.

"What the hell?" I squeal, pushing him back. "Why did you do that?"

He gives a half-shrug, seeming pretty damn pleased with himself. "You wanted proof. I figured that was the best way to give it to you."

"By licking me?"

"Yeah. Why not?"

I wipe my neck. "Because it's gross."

"Sure it is." And there's that smug smile again.

Screw him and his licking.

"Fine, if you don't think so, then I'm sure you won't mind me doing this." I raise my head and slide my tongue along his neck, making sure to drool a bit on his skin for good measure.

Instead of squealing, he curses, then licks my damn neck again.

"Stop!" I whine, but laughter is bursting from my lips.

I'm not even sure what the hell is so funny, yet I'm laughing like an idiot. I realize it's been a long time since I laughed this hard. I've been so stressed out lately. For years, actually.

Blaise is laughing, too, as he wipes his neck off.

"You're crazy."

"*I'm* crazy?" I work to calm my laughter. "You're the one who started a licking war. Who does that?"

"Why are you guys licking each other?" Alex's exhausted voice drifts from across the living room.

Blaise tenses then climbs off me, offering his hand to help me up. When I stand up without his help, he frowns, and I feel sort of bad, but I keep my apology to myself.

Sighing, he turns to Alex, who's leaning against the doorway, his eyelids half open, his skin pale.

"You finally decided to wake up, huh?" The playfulness in Blaise's demeanor is nonexistent as he stares at his brother.

Alex shrugs, rubbing his eyes with the heel of his hands. "Only because you two were being so damn loud."

"Good. I'm glad," Blaise snaps. "I've been here for over an hour trying to wake your ass up. I was one step away from carrying you out to the car."

Alex yawns, blinking his bloodshot eyes. "Why are you even here? I thought I messaged you not to come?" His gaze strays to me and narrows. "And why the hell is *she* here?"

"She was helping me this morning when Dad texted Rhyland to come get you." Blaise flexes his hands, struggling to keep his cool. "And you can try to text me all you want and tell me not to come get you, but I'm going to every time. You should know that by now."

"Only because you love being a pain in my ass." Alex clumsily strides toward him. "I don't get why you think you have any control over me. I'm almost eighteen; I can take care of myself."

"Yeah, obviously." Blaise's tone oozes sarcasm as he burns Alex with a look.

Alex slams his hands against Blaise's chest. "Fuck you, man. You don't know anything about me."

Blaise stumbles, the muscles in his jaw pulsating. "I know you're an addict."

"Fuck you," Alex seethes, getting in Blaise's face. "I can quit anytime I want. I just don't want to."

"You're so full of shit," Blaise seethes. "And I think deep down you know that."

"I'm not an addict," Alex's declares, his face reddening as his fingers curl into fists. "I choose to get high."

"If that's the case, then why?" Blaise's tone marginally softens. "Why are you choosing to slowly kill yourself?"

"That's none of your damn business," Alex mutters lowly. Then he steps back, raising his hands in front of him. "You know what? Fuck this. I'm getting another fix."

"Not an addict, huh?" Blaise challenges with a raise of his brow.

"I'm choosing to do this," Alex throws back as he hurries for the doorway. "I don't have to listen to you."

"Alex …" Blaise starts, chasing after him.

They disappear out of the room. Moments later, a door slams, followed by a lot of banging. Then silence.

I deliberate what to do, whether to go out to the car or not. I'd probably feel more awkward if I hadn't spent the last handful of years having similar arguments with my dad, sometimes in front of an audience.

After a minute ticks by, I slowly inch toward the doorway. "Blaise?"

A pause of silence, and then he mumbles shakily, "Yeah, just a sec."

I hesitantly peer around the corner.

He's standing just a ways down a dark hallway with his head resting against a door, his eyes shut, his body flowing with tension.

I almost turn around, let him have his meltdown, but … I don't know, sometimes, when I'm about to break apart, I secretly wish someone would help me hold it together. Not that I'd ever tell anyone that. Besides, the only people in my life who'd help me are the people I'd rather not see me have meltdowns.

Sucking in a breath, I start down the hallway toward him. "You okay?"

He unevenly inhales then lifts his head and faces me. "Yep, just great."

"You don't look great."

"I look how I always look."

"Then maybe you always don't look great."

"Wow, way to kick me when I'm down, Hadley," he tries to joke but misses the mark.

"I didn't mean it like that." I prop my shoulder against the wall. "I just meant that maybe you always look stressed out because you're always stressed out."

He laughs hollowly. "Stressed out? Is that what this is? Because I thought this constant helpless and irritated feeling festering inside me meant I had the best fucking life in the goddamned world … Shit." He turns away from me and lightly bangs his head against the door again. "I don't know why I keep telling you stupid shit. It was probably a really stupid idea to bring you here."

"Maybe," I agree. "But since I'm here, feel free to tell me stupid shit. It's nothing I haven't heard, or probably haven't said or thought myself."

He aims a skeptical look at me. "You've told a girl who hates your guts that you're stressed out all the time and secretly wish you lived alone instead of taking care of your brothers?" He whispers the last part.

"Not exactly."

He gives me a *see-I'm-right* look before lowering his forehead to the door again.

I drum my fingers against the sides of my legs, feeling restless and sorry for him. It's kind of annoying how much I want to make him feel better. I don't know why I feel this way. Maybe because I secretly wish I had someone to make me feel better? Or maybe I've just lost my damn mind. Who knows?

I stare at the cracked wall straight ahead of me that reminds me of so many of our old homes. "Hey, Blaise?"

"Yeah," he mumbles.

A shaky exhale escapes my lips. "I'm stressed out all the time. And I have these rules that … that are going to help me get the hell away from this life the moment I graduate, which is pretty shitty because that means I'm going to leave my sisters behind with our alcoholic, drug addict, con-man of a father who can't even take care of himself."

He gradually turns toward me, moving his head away from the door. He searches my eyes for an unnerving amount of time, so much so that I start to regret my confession.

"Rules?" he questions curiously. "What sort of rules?"

I shrug. "Nothing that interesting. Just keeping my grades up, keeping myself out of trouble, no dating—stuff like that."

He straightens, facing me fully now. "You have a no-dating rule? How does that help you with your plan?"

"Because guys are trouble." I shrug when he blasts me with a joking, dirty look. "What? They are."

"And you're not?"

"I never said that."

He shakes his head, gaping at me. "You're a really odd girl."

"You've said that, like, six times," I tell him. "It's starting to lose its dramatic effect."

He chuckles, his muscles loosening a bit. "Thank you."

My brows dip. "For what?"

"For ..." He scuffs the tip of his boot against the carpet. "For making me chill out, I guess."

"This is you chilled out?" I tease. "Wow, I'd hate to see you when you're really worked up."

He laughs, then faces the shut door again. "So damn weird." He plummets back into silence as he stares at the door. "I'm not sure what to do."

I push away from the wall and move up beside him. "With Alex?"

He nods, his gaze flitting to me. "I'm pretty sure he locked himself in there to shoot up again, which means, even if I pick the lock, he'll be passed out."

"Yeah, so? Just carry him out to the car."

"I would, but ..." He blows out a stressed breath. "I just feel like sometimes I'm enabling him by helping him."

"I can understand why you'd feel that way. I feel that way about my father sometimes."

He chews on his bottom lip. "What would you do in this situation?"

"Honestly?" I ask, and he nods. "Well, if it was my dad, I'd probably just leave his high-ass here. But only because he's really starting to wear on my nerves lately. Plus, he's been pulling shit like this for almost a decade, and we can't get him to get some help. If it was one of my sisters, though, I'd take them home, let the drugs wear out of their system, and then do whatever I could to either get them in rehab or get them some sort of help. But I love my sisters."

"You don't love your dad?"

"That's a complicated question."

"I can understand that. My dad's a real piece of work, but I'm sure you already know that." He doesn't wait for me to comment as he stares at the door again, drifting into silence. Then he mutters something under his breath, crouches, and examines the lock. "You have a hair pin or something that'll pick this?"

"Actually, I do." I reach up, remove a hairpin securing one of my braids, and hand it to him.

"You come prepared, huh?" he teases as he wiggles the pin into the lock.

"This isn't the first time I've had to help someone break into a room."

"Again, I'm not surprised." He twists the hair pin counterclockwise.

"You know, I feel like maybe I should feel insulted by your lack of surprise in my knowledge of criminal activities," I tease, slanting back with my boot propped up against the wall.

"But I doubt you will." The lock clicks, and then he pushes open the door and straightens.

"Nah, I probably won't. If I did, then I'd spend almost all my time feeling insulted." I reach to take the hair pin from him, but he tucks it back into my hair. Then he offers me a small smile before walking into the room.

My chest feels sort of weird in that moment. Fluttery. It makes me feel oddly unsettled and restless. Makes me want to smart off to him just to regain control over my body. But watching him cross the small room toward Alex, who is already passed out on a stained mattress with a band wrapped loosely around his arm, a needle beside his hand, I decide to keep my lips fused together.

"You need help carrying him out?" I ask as I step over the broken glass and garbage littering the room.

He shakes his head as he stands beside the mattress, staring down at his brother with pain, anger, and hurt crammed in his eyes. "Nah, I can get him."

"What can I do to help then?"

He casts a quick glance at me, his eyes searching mine, then he rubs his lips together and looks back at his brother. "Open the doors for me?"

"You got it." I kick the garbage and glass covering the floor out of the way with the tip of my boot as Blaise crouches and picks up Alex.

Alex's eyelids flutter, as if he's coming to. He mumbles something incoherently then stills again.

Blaise adjusts his weight then hikes across the room to where I'm standing. Neither of us exchange a word as I back out, head back across the living room, and open the front door.

Sunlight spills into the dusty room, along with fresh air. I breathe it in as I step out, realizing how damp and murky the air had been inside.

"Can you get the car door for me, too?" Blaise asks as he exits the house, squinting against the sunlight.

I nod then hurry to the SUV and open the back door.

Blaise gently sets Alex down on the back seat, shuts the door, and then we climb in. Again, quietness stretches between us as he starts up the engine and drives back the down the bumpy road.

"He's been through a lot of shitty stuffy," Blaise abruptly says as he pulls out onto the highway. "Alex, I mean." He flips down the visor then his guarded gaze lands on mine. "I know it's not an excuse for anything he does, but sometimes I wonder, if some of that shitty stuff never happened to him"—his eyes travel to the rearview mirror, to the reflection of his brother lying down in the back seat—"maybe he wouldn't be a drug addict who gets in trouble all the time and does crappy things to people who probably don't deserve it." His attention returns to the road, his shoulders stiffening. "Then again, maybe he'd still be the same. Who the hell knows?"

Just what sort of stuff has Alex been through? I won't ask, and not just because he probably won't tell me, but because it's none of my damn business. Not this. No, this is deeply personal, and I can respect his vagueness.

"Are you going to try to get him help?" I ask instead. "Maybe try to get him into a rehab facility?"

"I want to, but me wanting him to go and actually getting him to agree are two entirely different things." He cranks up the air conditioning. "But yeah, I'm going to try. My brothers and I, and even Scarlett, have been saving up money so we can give him an intervention and hopefully convince him to go." He hurriedly explains, "Scarlett's our half-sister. Have you met her? She doesn't live with us, but she stays over some weekends. You may have seen her around school."

"Yeah, I've seen her around a few times." I try to be as vague as possible, uncertain if Scarlett would want me confessing to Blaise that she was the one who told me about the dual. "And I think it's good that you're all working together to try to help Alex. I hope he does get help. Not just for his sake, but for you and your siblings, too."

His gaze flicks to mine. "You're very understanding about this."

I shrug. "I already told you that my dad does stuff like this all the time. And some of my sisters have, on occasion."

"I know, but ..." He stares at me, and I mean, really stares at me, in a way that makes me twitchy, as if he can actually see through the wall I constantly have around me. "I'm just not used to it—being around someone who's understanding. I mean, my siblings can be sometimes, but none of my friends have ever been this easy to talk to."

I squirm, even more uneasy now. "It's just because I've been through similar stuff, so I get it."

"I know." He continues to stare at me in that seeing, knowing, can't-really-breathe-properly way.

Finally, I decide I need a subject change before I end up diving out of the car just to avoid that look.

I rest my elbow on the back of the seat. "So, what do you guys do for work anyway? Because I find it hard as hell to get a job that pays decently and has flexible hours."

He studies me for a heartbeat longer before he tears his gaze away from me.

I secretly breathe in relief.

"Jax does work around the neighborhood, like mows lawns and stuff—I feel like he's too young to work more than that," he tells me. "Alex works at an auto shop. But the only reason he even has the job and hasn't gotten fired yet is because the owner of the shop is— was a friend of my mom's." He scratches his neck, visibly uncomfortable. "I work at the shop, too. Not on the cars, but in the office. Rhyland sometimes works there, but he makes most of his money racing."

"Wait. What?" That piques my interest. "How the hell does he make money racing?"

"People put up bets, and he makes a percentage." He glances at me with his brows knit. "Didn't they do that back in your hometown? I know you raced. Didn't you get money from doing it?"

I shake my head. "Not really, but I don't really have a

hometown. Maybe if we stayed put in the same place for longer than six months, I would've discovered the potential cash flow in something I love."

He gapes at me. "You move every six months?"

"Give or take a month."

"*Why?*"

I hesitate, questioning how much I should divulge. After all, my dad works for his dad, and telling Blaise the truth—that my dad generally tends to screw people over within that timeframe—doesn't seem like a great idea.

I settle on, "We just like a change of scenery, I guess."

Skepticism weighs in his eyes, but he drops the subject as we arrive at the outskirts of town and he turns into a gas station.

I check the time and frown. I'm two hours late for school already. *Crap.*

"Sorry, but the tank's already red lining," he apologizes as he notes me frowning at the clock. "I promise I'll hurry. And I can drop you off at school before I take Alex back to the house."

"It's fine. You can go home, and I can just drive myself to school … I don't want to make you drive to the school with him in the back seat like that"—I nod at Alex—"and risk getting pulled over or something."

"Are you sure?" he asks as he parks next to a pump.

"Yep, it's cool. Either way, I won't make it there until after lunch anyway."

He silences the engine then gives me a strange look. "Thanks, Hadley. What you did this morning ... and agreeing not to say anything ..." He clears his throat. "But yeah, thanks. I haven't felt this grateful in a very long time."

"No worries. It's not that big of a deal."

"Yeah, it really is." He *really* stares at me again. "Especially with how crappy I treated you when we first met and almost every time after that. I wish I hadn't, but ... yeah, I'm just sorry."

"No worries." As we start to share yet another moment, I bail out of the car. "I'm going to go get some coffee. You want anything?"

"I'm good, but thanks." His gaze remains glued on me, dissecting me.

"Okay." I shut the door and hightail it into the gas station, my heart racing in my chest. I don't know what the fucker's problem is today, but it needs to chill out. So what if Blaise isn't nearly as bad as I originally thought? My heart doesn't need to get all fluttery over it. It should be tougher than that.

I should be tougher than that.

"Remember the rules," I mutter to myself as I enter the gas station. "We don't need this getting out ..." I trail off as I spot my dad's truck through the window, parked in the side parking lot. A much nicer truck is parked beside it that has heavily tinted windows.

Curious as to what my dad is doing here in the middle of the day, I start to head back outside to ask, when the door to the nicer truck opens and my dad hops out. I pause, watching as he peers around nervously. Then he collects a large duffel bag from the truck, hurriedly climbs into his own truck, and then peels out of the parking lot, kicking up a cloud of dust.

I grind my teeth as I watch him speed off down the highway. "Another duffel bag, Dad? Really?"

I have a very suspicious and very unnerving feeling that the contents of that bag might be very similar to the bag buried in our backyard.

Just what the hell has my dad gotten mixed up in? And does this have anything to do with his new job?

My gaze floats over to where Blaise is standing next to his SUV. He's currently swiping his card in the machine, but his eyes are trained on the road, right in the direction my dad drove off in.

CHAPTER NINETEEN

I REMAIN FAIRLY STUCK IN MY OWN HEAD FOR MOST OF the remaining drive home, my mind crammed with questions. Questions about my dad. About what he was doing at the gas station with yet another duffel bag. Questions about Blaise. Like, how much he knows about my dad and about Blaise himself. The biggest question: what led him to seek guardianship of his brothers? What line was crossed that he finally decided they were better off without him?

How am I supposed to ask him any of this? I barely know him. He barely knows me. Why would he share his personal story with me? He may very well not, but at this point, I'm becoming desperate enough to ask.

I take a sip of my coffee then flick a quick glance to make sure Alex is still passed out before turning in the seat toward Blaise. He's hardly said more than a handful of words since we left the gas station, either stuck in his own head, too, or tired of chatting with me.

"I have to ask you a question."

Breaking the silence makes him jolt.

His gaze skates to me, his expression guarded. "Okay …?"

I finish off my coffee then set the empty cup in the cupholder. "You saw him at the gas station, didn't you?"

He reluctantly nods. "I saw him drive away."

"Do you know why he was there?"

"No."

I can't read him; can't tell if he's lying. "Was he there for his job?"

He shakes his head, sweeping strands of his blond hair out of his eyes. "Probably not."

"How do you know for sure? I mean, what does he even do for your dad?"

"All sorts of things. And I know for sure he wasn't working earlier because he only works nights."

"Nights? But sometimes I see him around the house at night."

"Late at night," he clarifies. "I think it's the eleven o'clock to five o'clock shift."

None of this makes sense, and with how much Blaise is squirming in his seat, I wonder if he knows more than he's letting on. But why? Because my dad told him not to tell me? Again, why?

Why? Why? Why?

"But he acts as if he's going to work during the day," I point out, observing his reaction closely. "He even packs a lunch."

Blaise thrums his fingers against the wheel, contemplating something. "Maybe he has two jobs?"

I snort a laugh. "Yeah, and unicorns are real."

He gives me a curious glance. "I'm guessing he's not the sort of guy who would have two jobs?"

"Hell no. He's not the type to even have one job. Honestly, until you said he was working for your dad, I thought he was just going to the bar with his"—I make air quotes—" 'lunchbox.' "

He nods understandingly. "I had one of those parents, too. Or, well, I should say stepparent." He downshifts as we near the turn off to our neighborhood. "Rhyland and Alex's mom … she's a real piece of work. And that's putting it mildly."

I seize the opportunity to ask, "Was she the reason you got guardianship of your brothers?"

"Partly." A tightness clenches his tone. "My father was the other reason." He flips on his blinker as he slows down to make a turn. "He was really pissed off at me at first. Or, well, pissed off is an understatement. But yeah, anyway, he was really pissed off until I made a valid point that, with the way things were going, we were probably going to get taken away from him anyway. Well, Alex, Jaxon, and Rhyland were. I was eighteen by then."

I realize something doesn't add up. "Wait. How long ago was this? I thought Rhyland said six months ago."

"I started the process about nine months ago. It took three months to get it done and probably would've taken longer if my dad hadn't decided to be cooperative." He presses his lips together, pausing. "I'm guessing by that confused look on your face that you're doing the math and realizing I'm almost nineteen yet still a senior in high school. That has nothing to do with me getting guardianship ... Back in sixth grade, I had to miss a year of school."

I almost ask what for, but he looks on the verge of being sick, his skin pale, his breathing increasing.

"So, your dad just gave you guardianship then?" I ask instead.

"After a bit of a fight, he did."

"Do you guys see him at all?"

"Occasionally, but we try to avoid it at all costs. Well, except for Alex ... but he doesn't always think clearly." His eyes travel to the rearview mirror. "I wish he would. The last thing I want is for him to get more mixed up in my dad's world ... It'll destroy him."

I recall how I overheard Blaise and Alex arguing last

night, how Alex declared he was torturing my sisters and me because someone fucked him over.

"Why did Alex go after my sisters and me?" I ask cautiously. "Was it just because of what I said to you the first time we met? Or is there more to it than that?"

"Alex barely had any involvement in that," he lies flatly. "It was mostly me."

"If you say so."

"I do say so."

"Okay."

He nearly growls. "You're so frustrating sometimes. Seriously, are you always like this?"

"Yeah, pretty much," I admit truthfully. "But, FYI, you're equally as annoying. And I know for a fact that you had nothing to do with my tires getting slashed or the flyers. But it's cool. I get you're trying to protect your brother, so I'll let it drop."

He assesses me with his lips pressed together as he steers up his driveway. "I can't figure you out at all. I mean, you can be rude and intense and maybe even slightly crazy, yet you've been so understanding with stuff, and you're just ..." He shakes his head. "I don't get you."

I stay put despite how badly I want to dive out of the car. But he's got that stupid look on his face again, the one where I'm pretty sure he can see through my layer that I keep hidden.

"Most people can't, so you should probably just stop trying to do it."

He shakes his head, not saying a word as he pushes the shifter into park, neither agreeing nor denying with my request, leaving me to wonder.

I really need to stop wondering about him.

"Are you sure you don't want me to drive you to school?" he asks, glancing at his brother. "I can hurry and put him inside then drive you, if you need me to?"

"Nah, I can drive myself. I'm not a very good passenger anyway. I like to be behind the wheel too much." I try for a smile to lighten the mood, but this ride has been too intense and I'm not really feeling it.

Blaise seems on the same page, offering me only a stiff smile.

"All right," he says, making no move to get out.

"Okay."

I tell myself to get out of the car, but instead, I just end up staring at him, wondering, wondering, wondering.

Wondering way too much about him.

As awkwardness stretches between us, I find myself missing arguing with him again. At least then I didn't feel so out of my element.

Throwing him a quick grin, I jump out and hurry toward the fence, feeling weirded out. I try to blame it on lack of sleep, but the truth is Blaise got me all baffled and confused. My first initial assessment of him feels way off now. Still, I can't get past the first time I met him.

How can that cocky jerk be the guy who just opened up to me? Or who takes care of his drugged-out brother?

As I make my way up my driveway and toward my car, I watch out of the corner of my eye as Blaise opens the back door of the SUV, gently picks up his brother, and carries him toward the house.

Who is Blaise Porterson? And, can I trust him?

Part of me says yes, but the other part—the part that believes he knows more about my dad's job than he's letting on—cautions me to be careful.

CHAPTER TWENTY

I ARRIVE AT SCHOOL RIGHT AROUND THE TIME LUNCH ends, so I have no time to talk to my sisters. After I check in with the office, giving them a forged note excusing my absence, I hurry to class to avoid being late again. Since I missed fifth period yesterday, I ask the teacher what I missed. Then I take a seat in the farthest row back, hoping to keep my head down and avoid the gawking, because apparently, people haven't gotten over the whole flyer thing yet.

"Hey." Rhyland drops his books on the desk in front of mine then plops down in the seat. "You made it?"

"Yeah, just barely." I dig a pen out of my bag then straighten in the seat, too aware that the gawking around me has increased since Rhyland started talking to me. "Hey, thanks for giving my sisters a ride this morning. That was really … nice of you."

"Nice?" He smiles amusedly. "Wow, did I just get a compliment from you?"

I shrug. "I give compliments occasionally."

"Yeah, but you seem like a hard girl to win over, so it kind of feels like, I don't know, an honor or something."

"It is." I can't help smiling when he grins at me. "But being a hard girl to win over isn't a bad thing."

"I know. But you need to let people win you over sometimes; or else, how are people supposed to get to know you?"

My smile withers. "Sometimes it's easier not to."

He pauses for a beat. "You sound a lot like my brother."

My lips dip downward. "Which one?"

"Blaise." He searches my eyes. "Was that the answer you were hoping for or not? I can't tell."

Shrugging, I relax back in my seat. "There could be worse answers, I guess."

He chuckles softly, but his laughter hastily fades as he sneaks a glance around the room. Then he lowers his voice. "How did it go this morning with Blaise? He hasn't texted me yet. Did he make it to school?"

Remembering how Blaise mentioned his siblings not knowing how bad Alex has gotten, I decide to be as vague as possible. "This morning went okay. We picked up Alex, got gas and stuff, then he dropped me off at my car. He didn't come to school, though. Said he has some stuff to do or something."

"Oh." His lips thin as he presses them together. "Alex was okay, though?"

"He seemed okay," I lie again, wishing I asked Blaise what I was supposed to tell everyone this morning. It's the first rule of telling a believable lie: make sure your stories line up. "I actually didn't talk to him too much. Alex, I mean. In case you haven't heard, he's not a huge fan of me." The last part comes off teasing.

Sometimes I'm such a fantastic liar that I freak myself out. I didn't used to be this way. Before my mom died, I cried every time I tried to lie. My parents used to laugh at me, saying I was going to turn into the most honest person in the world with how terrible of a liar I was. And look at me now. I can lie without missing a beat and rarely does anyone get to know the real me.

Rhyland sighs. "He does seem to have some sort of vendetta against you, doesn't he? That's just Alex. All of us Portersons have our one quirk that rubs people the wrong way."

"Just one?" I question.

He chuckles, his eyes crinkling around the corners. "Okay, maybe we have more, but not all of them are completely bad." He rests his arms on top of my desk. "We have good traits, too."

I toss a glance at the people openly staring at us. "And are people staring at us because of your good traits or your bad ones?"

He peers around the room, his mouth curving downward as his eyes land back on me. "It's probably because of both." He fiddles with a leather band on his wrist. "Some people fear us because of our last name. Some people want us because of who we are. Honestly, either way, we have a hard time trusting people. It's why Jaxon barely talks to anyone, why we don't have any close friends, why we rarely date."

A soft laugh escapes me. "I have a hard time believing the last one."

When his gaze lifts to mine, curiosity sparkles in his eyes. "Why not?"

"I don't know. Maybe because everything about all of you—well, except for maybe Jaxon—screams player."

He presses his hand to his chest, mocking offense. "I am so not a player. I barely flirt with anyone."

"Liar. You flirted with me the first time we met." Despite my seriousness, I'm on the verge of laughing.

"I mildly flirted with you," he corrects, grinning. "And I backed off, didn't I?"

"Sort of. But I'm guessing only because Blaise made you."

"There might be a little truth to that statement. How did you know?"

"It's pretty obvious."

He bobs his head up and down. "Yeah, my brother's never been that subtle, I guess."

"Yeah, I could tell that from the first time I met him and he tried to hit on me. He has the worst moves ever. How he's ever gotten a date is beyond me."

Rhyland barks out a laugh, causing even more people to stare at us. "Jesus, you're amusing," he says through his laughter.

As the bell rings and the teacher starts to call roll, I slant forward and whisper, "Why's that so funny?"

Tears of laughter glimmer in his eyes. "I was just picturing Blaise actually going out on a date and trying to ask a girl out."

Confusion tap dances inside my mind. "You say that like he's never dated."

"That's because he hasn't," he says in all seriousness. "Not really anyway."

I think back to how he acted like such a player—my initial assumption of him. "Does he know that? Because he acts the opposite."

He scans me over with intrigue. "Just what exactly has been going on between my brother and you?"

I chew on the end of my pen. "You should know. You've been there for most of it."

"Not the first time you met."

"That was probably the worst."

"Why?" He's even more intrigued.

"Um, because he called me *baby* and *sweetheart*, and then acted like an asshole when I told him a very colorful way to go fuck himself. It was like no one had ever told him off before."

"That's because people rarely do. It's the curse of our last name," he explains while struggling not to laugh. "I don't know what's funnier—you telling Blaise off, or Blaise trying to flirt with you? I'm not sure I've ever seen him flirt with anyone."

"Are you being serious right now? Because what you're saying and what I've seen doesn't match. So far, Blaise seems like an asshole." Well, minus some parts from today.

"I think you—"

"Rhyland, please turn around in your seat," the teacher interrupts before Rhyland can answer.

Shrugging, Rhyland faces forward, but not before whispering, "You should cut Blaise some slack, Hadley. He's had a rough life and rarely lets people in. But the people he does let in are really lucky. Trust me."

He leaves it at that, only adding to my developing confusion of who Blaise really is. It shouldn't matter to me. If I was sticking to my rules, it wouldn't. But apparently, within the course of two weeks of living in

Honeyton, I've managed to veer off course and lose focus on what's important. And that can't happen. Ever. I need to stay focused, not just for my sake, but for my sisters'. That means no more thinking or worrying about Blaise.

CHAPTER TWENTY-ONE

My sisters are surprisingly upbeat as we drive home from school. I assumed, since people hadn't let up with the whole flyer incident, that they'd be mopey and in desperate need of some ice cream. Instead, they're all giggles and jokes and chatting about hot guys.

"Speaking of who's hot …" Payton slides forward in the back seat and rests her arms on the console. "How was your morning with our sexy next-door neighbor?"

So much for not thinking about Blaise. "I'm assuming you mean Blaise?"

"Well, sexy could describe any of them," she says, "but yeah, I'm talking about Blaise. Unless you spent the morning with more than one Porterson?"

"Actually, Alex was with us," I tell her, only because I already told Londyn.

Payton crinkles her nose. "God, I feel so bad for you. He's so annoying. I've heard a lot of other people say terrible stuff about him."

"He's got quite the rep for being a douchebag," Bailey agrees. "The rest of Portersons don't seem so bad. Well, Rhyland and Jaxon don't. I know you hate Blaise, even if you two did kiss the shit out of each other."

Payton snickers. "Hell yeah, they did."

"No, we didn't," I protest, knowing I'm so full of it. That kiss yesterday was hot, just like that whole licking thing that happened between us, which FYI, I am never telling my sisters about. They'd never let it go.

"Sure, you didn't," Bailey singsongs, perfectly in pitch.

"It's okay if you did," Londyn reassures me from the passenger seat. She has a soccer ball on her lap and is twisting her hair up into a messy bun. "I know I said a lot of crap about them the other day, but I think I've decided not all the Portersons are bad. Alex is not included in that assessment. And Blaise … I'm still undecided about him. He seemed like such a jerk when we first met him, and then that stupid bet … But I don't know if I'm right or not." She looks at me for my opinion.

"He might not be as bad as he seemed at first. And the bet, that was partially my doing," I say as I speed up to pass a car. "Plus, I think he was the one who bought me the new tires."

Londyn's jaw basically ninja slaps her lap. "Seriously?"

I nod, shifting gears. "Yeah, I overheard him talking to Alex about it. I guess Alex was the one who slashed my tires and Blaise bought the replacements." I purposefully don't mention when I overheard this conversation, hoping to avoid talking about the bag buried in the backyard, since that will only lead to me lying more.

"Then, why did Blaise act like he was the one who slashed them?" she wonders, dropping her soccer ball onto the floor.

"I think because Alex gets into so much trouble," I tell her. "He's trying to protect him or something."

She aims a purposeful glance at my neck where my necklace once was. "That sounds familiar."

My hand floats to the base of my neck. "I guess so … But anyway …" I lower my hand and change the subject, not wanting to talk about Mom's necklace. Or for Bailey and Payton to find out that I pawned it. "The tire thing was pretty cool of Blaise. And he didn't really seem too bad this morning. I mean, don't get me wrong, he still got under my skin, but he wasn't as terrible as I thought he was going to be. I'm still trying to figure him out—if he's really a nice guy and my first impression of him was wrong, or if he's just putting on an act now. According to Rhyland, Blaise isn't cocky at all. And he says he doesn't usually hit on girls or date, so I don't get why Blaise was trying all that *sweetheart, baby* flirty crap the first time we met …" I trail off as I become highly aware they are all staring at me in amusement. "Why are you guys looking at me like that? What's so damn funny about what I said?"

Londyn slowly shakes her head as she stares off into empty space. "It's nothing." She then trades a smile with Bailey and Payton.

"It's something," I scoff. "Or else you guys wouldn't be grinning at each other like a couple of silly Muppet babies."

Bailey giggles. "We're Muppet babies."

I sigh. "Come on; just tell me."

"It really is nothing." Londyn pulls out a pack of gum from her bag, pops a piece in her mouth, and then props her feet on the dash as she sits back. "We've just never heard you talk about a guy so much. You're usually so anti-guys."

"Because guys are trouble." Irritation burns inside me at her speculation. I'm mostly irritated with myself, because she's right. "And I'm only talking about Blaise because you guys were asking me questions about him."

"Okay." Doubt laces her tone, which only frustrates me more.

"It's the truth." I turn into our empty driveway. *So, Dad's not home yet.* "You guys brought Blaise up first when you asked me how my morning went with him."

"True." Londyn nods in agreement then glances over at the Portersons' driveway where their SUV and Rhyland's car is parked.

Rhyland is getting out. He throws us a wave while Jaxon hops out and scrambles up to the house without a glance in our direction.

"He was so offish on the drive to school this morning," Bailey remarks as she slings her backpack over her shoulder.

"I think he's just shy." Payton's eyes remain on Jaxon until he disappears into the house.

I slip the keys out of the ignition and open the door. "How did your drive with them go this morning anyway? Londyn said not too bad."

Bailey stuffs her phone into her pocket. "It was okay."

"Much better than I thought it was going to be," Payton agrees as Londyn gets out and flips up the seat to let her out. "When Londyn first accepted Blaise's offer to ride with them, I nearly shit a brick."

"Me, too," Bailey says as I hop out and slide the seat forward. "I'm sure if Alex was with us, things would've been awful. It just sucks that you had to spend the morning with him." She offers me an apologetic look as she ducks out of the car.

"Actually, he was pretty quiet for the most part." I can feel all their gazes on me as I make my way up the driveway, probably wanting more of an explanation. But I promised Blaise. And while I can be a straight-up liar about a lot of things, I respect—and understand—his need to protect his brother way too much. So, I shrug when I reach the front door and see they still haven't stopped staring at me. "What? He was."

The three of them trade yet another glance, and then Londyn's gaze zeroes in on me. "What're you not telling us?"

I avoid their gazes as I unlock the door. "I'm not keeping anything from you. Why would you ask that?"

Her gaze is relentless. She knows me too well. "Because I know you, and I can tell you are."

"I'm really not." I'm so torn. Torn over telling her the truth and keeping my promise to Blaise. "I don't know why it seems that way."

She stares at me for a bit longer before looking away with hurt in her eyes. "All right." Then she steps inside the house and heads straight up to our bedroom.

Releasing a sigh, I move to chase after her so I can tell her … well, I'm not certain yet, but then our dad pulls into the driveway and my worries transfer elsewhere.

I step back outside onto the porch. "Hey, Bay, Payton, can you guys go up to your room for a bit? I need to have a chat with Dad."

"About the alcohol he buried in the backyard?" Bailey glances at our dad's truck.

"Yeah." Another lie. At this point, I've told so many I'm starting to get tangled up in them. "Well, that and a couple other things."

"Good." With a firm nod, she goes inside.

Payton follows, patting me on the shoulder. "Don't go easy on him, Had," she encourages. "He doesn't deserve it."

"Oh, I won't," I swear. When she shoots me an unconvinced frown, I stress, "I know I've gone easy on him in the past, but I'm at my final straw. It's time he understands that we're not going to put up with any more of his shit."

Her lack of confidence in me decreases a notch. "Good. And if you need any help, shout for us, okay? Don't let him bully you into backing off."

"All right." But I'm not about to bring them into this. As the oldest, my job is to protect them. To keep them away from our dad. To make sure they're safe. To make sure they're happy, even if it means giving them some of my happiness.

My attention briefly strays to the Porterson house.

Does Blaise ever feel this way? Like he's okay with being less happy as long as his siblings are content?

I instantly shake my head. Why, oh, why did I start thinking about him again?

Get him out of your damn head, woman!

Shifting my focus off Blaise's house, I trot down the steps and approach my dad's truck. He's sitting in the driver's seat, distracted by his phone. The duffel bag I saw him collect earlier is on the passenger seat.

When he remains oblivious to me standing there, I tap my knuckles against the window. He jumps so badly he drops his phone.

"Shit." He hastily collects his phone from the floor and straightens in his seat, blinking at me. "Hadley, where'd you come from?"

"The house." I hitch my thumb over my shoulder. "Didn't you see me walking down the driveway?"

He shakes his head then rolls the window down all the way. "But, what're you doing at home?" His puzzled expression alters into a scowl. "Wait. You aren't cutting out on class, are you?"

"Like you'd care if I was. You never have before," I say bitterly. "And no, I'm not cutting." I don't offer a further explanation as I open the truck door. "You and I need to talk."

He has the audacity to appear perplexed. "About what?"

"About the bag you buried in the backyard." I glance at the bag on the seat. "And that one right there, too, if it has the same contents as the one in the backyard."

His eyes fleetingly widen, but then he narrows them into slits. "How many times have I told you to stay out of my goddamn business?"

I lean in closer, lowering my tone. "When your goddamn business could get you arrested and Child Protective Services called, then it becomes my goddamn business."

"Shut your fucking mouth," he hisses, glancing around in a panic. "And stay out of my fucking business."

I shake my head. "No, I'm not going to this time. I've had enough. I had enough a long time ago, actually—ever since Mom died—but I let you get away with a lot of shit because I felt sorry for you. That was my mistake. I'm not going to do it anymore."

"What exactly are you trying to say?" His tone is like ice.

"That if you don't cut this shit out"—I point at the backyard and nod at the bag—"then I'm going to try to gain guardianship of my sisters. I'm eighteen now, and I know, under the right circumstances, I can get it."

"You can't do that," he warns lowly, turning in his seat. "Again, you're forgetting who the parent is. Those are my daughters in that house. A house I pay for us to live in." He grinds his teeth. "And you're my daughter, too, even though I wish you weren't right now."

My heart squeezes in my chest, but I shove my walls up.

Don't let him get to you. Don't feel a thing.

"I …" That's when I smell the whiskey on his breath. I shake my head. "Great, you're drunk, and you've been driving around town. Awesome parenting example, Dad."

"I just had one drink," he snaps, the vein in his neck bulging. "And what I do as a parent is none of your business."

"It is, too, my damn business!" My voice is rising as my temper gets the best of me. "You can't just do whatever you want and think it's not going to affect us! Because it does! All the time! You don't pay the bills, you don't take care of us, and you haven't since Mom died. And if she were here, she'd be so disappointed in you—"

He lunges from the truck and strikes me across the face so hard my ears ring.

I move back, cupping my cheek, when he comes at me again, this time bringing his hand down on top of my head. My teeth clank together as tears sting my eyes and blood drips from my nose. Shock whips through me.

Holy shit, he's going to beat the shit out of me.

He comes at me again with his fist raised, but stumbles, giving me just enough time to swing around him.

I start to take off up the driveway when he grabs my hair. I let out a cry, more tears falling from my eyes. I'm not even sure if the tears are from the pain in my body or my heart. I don't even care anymore.

Balling my hand into a fist, I swing at him, my knuckles colliding with his shoulder. He grunts, but then yanks on my hair harder.

"Goddamn, Hadley, why can't you just let this go!" he screams out. "You don't even know what you're messing with!"

"A monster!" I shout as I grab his hand and try to pry his fingers off my hair. "Let me go!" I scream.

More screams echo. Not mine.

I glance toward the house and spot Londyn striding forward. Payton and Bailey are by the side door, Payton holding Bailey back with tears streaming down her eyes.

"Let her go!" Londyn shouts at our dad.

Either he doesn't hear her, or he's lost his mind, because he only yanks on my hair harder and spins me around toward the truck.

"No!" he yells, his grip constricting. "You couldn't just leave me alone. Why can't you just leave me alone?" His voice catches.

I think he might be crying, yet he still doesn't release my hair.

"Mel, let her go." The firm voice belongs to a guy, but it takes my wired mind a second to connect a face to it.

Blaise.

"Stay out of this," my dad snaps at him. "This is none of your business."

"Do I need to remind you who my father is?" Blaise asks calmly as he hoists himself over the fence and lands in our yard. Then he stalks toward us, taking measured steps. "Now, let go of Hadley, get in the truck, and get the fuck out of here before I call the cops."

"Too late." Londyn moves up beside Blaise, her wide eyes fixed on me and Dad. "I already called them."

"Shit," my dad and I say at the same time.

My dad quickly releases my hair and dives into his truck, slamming the door. I start to storm after him—no way am I letting him just take off and leave this mess to me—but arms are wrapped around me, holding me back.

"Just let him go," Blaise says softly in my ear. "It's better if he's gone."

"I don't want him here"—tears fall from my eyes, but my tone is so hollow—"but if he's not, my sisters are going to get taken away from me. He needs to give me guardianship first." I'm about to crumble, fall to pieces that I may never be able to pick up.

I suck in a breath. Then another.

Don't fall to pieces, Hadley. Keep it together.

Then I hear the sirens, and I damn near collapse.

"I'll help you," Blaise whispers, holding me up. "But you have to keep your shit together, okay? They'll probably take your sisters for a little bit, but I can help you get them out. I promise."

I nod, hoping to God I can trust him.

At this point, I'm not sure if I'll ever trust anyone again.

CHAPTER TWENTY-TWO

LIKE I EXPECTED, SOCIAL SERVICES SHOW UP TO TAKE MY sisters to a group home while I get patched up in the ambulance and answer an officer's questions.

Watching my sisters get hauled away in tears, I hate my father in that moment, more than I ever have, even more than when he was hurting me. What makes me feel even more crappy is I should've seen this coming. Maybe I did. Maybe I was just living in denial.

"I swear to the moon and back I'll fix this!" I shout to my sisters as the car they were put in starts to drive away. I stand up from the back of the ambulance, letting the blanket wrapped around my shoulders fall to the ground. "I swear to the moon and back I will."

Londyn watches me through the back window until she can no longer see me, until I can no longer see her.

Another officer approaches me then and asks even more questions, most of which are about what happened and my dad, like if I know where he went—stuff like that. By the time everyone clears out, my dad is now a wanted man, my sisters are gone, and the blood on my face has dried. My heart, though, still feels like it's bleeding.

"So." Blaise steps up beside me as the last officer pulls away.

He's been hanging around the entire time, answering questions. It's late. The sun set behind the shallow hills hours ago, and the air has a slight nip to it, yet I don't feel cold. Numbness. That's all I feel.

"So," I mimic as I stand near the side door, staring down the empty driveway.

I should go inside, take a shower, and wash the blood off my face, but I'm not that eager to greet the darkness and stillness awaiting me inside.

"Hadley." He gently places a hand on my shoulder.

I tense—I don't even know why—and he quickly removes his hand.

"I should go inside." I start to turn, but he steps in front of me.

"The paramedics said you might have a concussion." He levels his gaze with mine. "I think you should sleep over at my house for the night so you're not alone. I can sleep on the couch, and you can take my bed."

"I'm fine." *Lie*. I'm not even close to being fine. *I'm broken.*

He eyes me over with doubt. "Even if you are, it's still a good idea for you not to be alone. The paramedics even said so; said someone should keep an eye on you."

"And you want to be that person?" I question in disbelief.

He shrugs, stuffing his hands into his pockets. "I don't mind doing it."

"You should. You barely know me. And I'm the one who owes you favors, not the other way around."

He chews on his bottom lip as he stares at me strangely. "Yeah, I know, but I still want you to stay over at my house for the night, just until we know for sure if you're concussed. Then tomorrow, we'll make a plan on how we're going to get your sisters back."

He keeps throwing around the word *we*, and my initial instinct is to correct him, but I feel too disheartened to start bantering with him, so I simply nod and say, "All right, let me just grab some clothes first." I head into the house, but when he trails after me, I pause. "Can I just have a few minutes? I promise I'll come over as soon as I get my stuff."

He dithers then nods. "Sure."

I offer him what is probably the most miserable yet grateful smile then dash into the house.

The moment the door shuts, I collapse to the floor and cry for five minutes straight. That's all the time I give myself—five minutes to break the fuck down. Then I dry my eyes and pull myself together, vowing to never break down again. To be strong. Because, if I'm ever going to have a chance to get guardianship of my sisters, that's who I need to be.

Strong.

CHAPTER TWENTY-THREE

After I grab my pajamas, I go over to the Portersons' house like I said I would, where Blaise is waiting for me. Their house is surprisingly quiet.

"Alex is still sleeping it off," Blaise explains as he leads me up a stairway to his room. "And Jaxon and Rhyland are in their rooms, playing video games. No one will bother you, I promise." He points to a cracked open door as we pass it. "That's the bathroom, if you need to use it." He stops in front of a shut door and opens it. "And here's my room." He motions me inside.

I step in, noting the space is shockingly clean. The bed is made, there are no clothes on the floor, and there's minimal clutter.

"Are you a neat freak?" I ask.

He slants against the doorframe with his hands in

his pockets. "No, not really. I actually hurried up and cleaned it before you came over here. Kicked a lot of stuff under the bed and tossed the rest in the closet."

I laugh softly, and a small smile touches his lips. "That sounds like something Payton would do."

"What about you?" he asks. "Are you a neat freak?"

I shake my head, tucking a strand of hair behind my ear. "But I clean a lot. Not because I want to, but because, if I don't, no one else will."

"Me, too. That's probably why my room's so messy —I never have time to clean it. My brothers are slobs. I swear they think the floor is a trash can or something."

I smile, but this time the move is more forced. Talking about cleaning and his brothers is reminding me too much of my sisters.

"I should probably get to bed," I say. "It's been a … well, I'm not really sure what to call today."

He nods, understanding, and starts to back out. "Of course."

Something dawns on me. Or, well, I realize I need to say something.

"Blaise," I say quietly.

He pauses. "Yeah?"

"Thank you for what you did tonight."

His lips tilt into a small smile. "You're welcome. And if you need anything else at all, I'll be downstairs on the sofa, okay?" He waits for me to nod then closes the door, whispering, "Goodnight, stubborn girl."

And the nicknames are back. But I'm not as annoyed as I usually am.

As silence surrounds me, tears threaten to pour out, but I blink until they vanish. Then I put on my pajamas and climb into bed.

The blanket I pull over me smells like Blaise's cologne. I didn't even realize I knew what his cologne smelled like until now. It's a nice smell. I breathe it in as I roll over and try to get comfortable in Blaise's bed, something I never thought I'd be doing.

He surprised me today, and not just tonight when he stopped my dad from hurting me, but earlier today. I don't know what to make of that—make of him—but I'm fairly convinced that the cocky guy I first met by the fence isn't who Blaise really is.

I'm glad he's helping me, but that doesn't mean I'm going to allow myself to rely on him. No, I'll never be that girl. And not just because of my rules.

Fuck, my rules. They probably can't even exist anymore, can they? Not with me deciding to pursue guardianship of my sisters.

Reality crashes down on me, heavy and throbbing, just like my injured face. My rules don't—can't exist anymore. My future plans are gone. Nothing will ever be the same for me. But that doesn't mean I'm just going to walk away from this. I knew the moment Social Services drove away with my sisters that I need them in my life. That I can't let us be separated. That I'm going to have to step up. That that's what our mom would've wanted me to do.

"You're the bravest of my daughters," she used to say to me. "Fearless. It's why I know you'll make a great racer someday. You're going to make me proud; I just know it."

She was right. I am fearless and brave and a damn good racer. I just hope I can make her proud.

As I lie in bed, my eyelids growing heavy, that's what I think about—making my mom proud. And thinking of her relaxes me. If only the feeling could've carried into my dreams …

I'm standing near the street with a river flowing on one side, the sound of car engines filling the air. Then I hear tires skidding, followed by a loud splash.

"No!" my dad shouts from beside me. Then he rushes toward the river, leaving me behind with a mob of bystanders.

I start to run after him, but then my stomach clenches as someone screams.

No, not someone. I'm screaming, because someone is gripping my arms and dragging me back, away from my dad, away from the accident, away from my mom.

I scream again when a hand clamps down over my

mouth. "Quiet," the person warns. "Everything will be fine as long as your dad pays his debt."

Then I'm picked up and hauled away into the dark—

My eyes pop open, and I bolt upright, gasping for air.

"Holy shit," I breathe out, my heart a racing mess. "Where the hell did that dream come from?"

Or was it a dream? Because the images ... they felt so real. But, wouldn't I remember if I was taken? That's something you don't just forget. Then again, it was eight years ago, and I have those blank memories where the days between my mom's death and her funeral should be.

I cup the side of my face where my cheek throbs with the reminder of what my dad did to me only hours ago. I had thought he was just starting to turn into a monster, but what if it's been building over time?

"What did you do, Dad?" I whisper. "What did you do?"

My only answer is silence. That doesn't mean I'm going to let it stay that way. I will find out the truth, no matter what.

CHAPTER 24

BLAISE

Instead of going downstairs right away, I linger. It makes me nervous that she has a concussion. Plus, her dad is out wandering around, and who knows if he'll return? It's not just that that has me worried, though. No, it's the people her dad's gotten mixed up with. Like my dad, for starters.

Yes, he's my father, but that man is corrupt, and so is anyone who works for him. Hadley's dad isn't technically working for him, though. He's just working off a gambling debt that he's owed for over a decade now. He's lucky my dad let him off that easy and gets to work as his little bitch. Normally, when someone owes my dad money, especially for that amount of time, things don't end well for the debtor.

I'm not sure why he let Hadley's dad off so easily. I could ask, but my dad and I rarely talk, and when we do, he usually tells me nothing but bullshit lies. The best day of my life was when I got guardianship of my brothers and we were no longer obligated to talk to him. Well, not as much anyway. A monthly visit was his stipulation before he signed over guardianship to me.

When I'm almost certain Hadley is asleep, I do a quick sweep through of the house, making sure all the doors are locked. Next, I peer out the window, looking out at the street, frowning at the car parked near the corner.

The tinted windows and luxury are a giveaway that the owner more than likely doesn't live around here. My bet is it's the other people Hadley's dad has gotten mixed up with, something I discovered today while we were at the gas station and I saw Mel in one of Axel's men's truck.

Axel is my dad's rival who does a lot of dealings in drugs and runs some gambling sites. Yeah, Honeyton's really corrupt, mostly because the people who taint the town are rich enough to buy off the police, my dad and Axel being two of them.

If my dad finds out Mel is working for him, there's going to be hell to pay. And he may not just go after Mel.

Since the person currently parked outside is either one of my dad's men or Axel's—I'm betting the latter—that means Mel may have pissed off Axel. That man seems to have a knack for that. He seems to have a knack for doing a lot of shitty things, like beating his daughter.

My jaw twitches as I remember how angry I felt when I saw him hitting Hadley. It reminded me too much of when my dad hit my mom.

I heard a scream first and looked out the window. Then I saw red and heard nothing but my blood roaring in my heart. I probably would've beat Mel's ass if he hadn't bailed like a fucking coward.

How he managed to raise someone like Hadley doesn't make any sense. The girl is tough as hell and strong, and not just physically. Most people would've broken the fuck down tonight, yet she held it together. Underneath that tough exterior, though, she's got to be hurting. I know because I've been there, especially when my mom died. And whenever I'm around my father, but that's for a different reason.

I stay near the window until the car drives away. Then I lie down on the sofa, but I don't doze off right away, my mind in worry mode.

I think about Alex and how I'm going to convince him to get away from our father's world and into rehab.

I also worry over Jaxon and if he's ever going to get over this no-talking thing, something that started right after our mom died. Rhyland's probably the easiest, but his racing concerns me. He's getting more and more reckless every day. Scarlett's a handful, too, but she's only here some weekends. She mostly lives with her mom, though her mom's new drug addiction is starting to make me question if perhaps she should be living with us full-time.

Yeah, my life is full of stress. Now even more so.

Hadley, Hadley, Hadley. She's stuck in my mind. I want to help her get her sisters back, yet I'm not sure how I'm going to do that, or how I'll balance helping everyone out. I barely have time as it is. But something about Hadley feels oddly familiar, and not just because she reminds me of myself. I'm unsure where the familiarity comes from.

The first day I saw her, I knew she was different from other girls. Hot as hell, for sure, and her toughness turns me on, even if that makes me fucking twisted. And that kiss ... it was hands down the best fucking kiss I've ever had. Well, up until she kicked me in the dick. That part sucked big time.

I guess I sort of deserved it in a way, for being an ass to her when I first met her. But I was trying to protect Alex. Well, that and I suck at flirting. Rhyland's always giving me shit about having no game. He's right, but I spent most of my teenage years trying to be a parent. Even before I got guardianship, I took care of my brothers and my sister.

"You okay?" Rhyland asks as he wanders into the living room.

I nod, stretching out on the sofa. "Just trying to sleep."

He plops down on the chair across from me. "Hadley's staying in your room?"

I nod through a yawn. "It didn't seem like a good idea for her to stay in that house alone."

"I completely agree with you." He kicks his feet up onto the coffee table. "I'm a little worried about you, too. You're taking too much on."

"I'm fine."

"You always say that."

"That's because I always am."

He sighs as he slumps back in the chair. "You know, it's weird, but I swear she seems familiar."

I turn on my side to look at him. "Who does?"

"Hadley." He shrugs, while I pull my brows together. "I don't know why, but it feels like I've met her before."

"Yeah, me, too," I mumble.

"Really?" he asks, and I nod. "That's kind of weird."

"I'm sure we're just being weird," I say. Still, I can't

shake the feeling that maybe he's right. Perhaps I have met Hadley before. But when?

I guess it doesn't really matter right now. All that does is getting Alex help, keeping my siblings out of trouble, and helping Hadley get her sisters back. I just hope I can handle everything.

ABOUT THE AUTHOR

About the Author

Jessica Sorensen is a *New York Times* and *USA Today* bestselling author who lives in the snowy mountains of Wyoming. When she's not writing, she spends her time reading and hanging out with her family.

Curse of the Vampire Queen:

Tempting Raven

Enchanting Raven

Alluring Raven

Untitled (coming soon)

Mystic Willow Bay Witches Series:

The Secret Life of a Witch

Broken Magic

Stolen Kisses (coming soon)

Standalones:

The Forgotten Girl

The Honeymoon Series:

The Illusion of Annabella

Rebels & Misfits:

Confessions of a Kleptomaniac

Rules of a Rebel and a Shy Girl

The Fareland Society:

The Opposite of Ordinary

Untitled (coming soon)

<u>**Broken City Series:**</u>

Nameless

Forsaken

Oblivion

Forbidden (coming soon)

<u>**Guardian Academy Series:**</u>

Entranced

Entangled

Enchanted

The Forest of Shadow and Bones

Entice

Charmed

Untitled (coming soon)

<u>**Sunnyvale Series:**</u>

The Year I Became Isabella Anders

The Year of Falling in Love

The Year of Second Chances

The Year of Kai & Isa

Untitled (coming soon)

<u>**Unraveling You Series:**</u>

Unraveling You

Raveling You

Awakening You

Inspiring You

Every Single Breath

Untitled (coming soon)

The Coincidence Series:

The Coincidence of Callie and Kayden

The Redemption of Callie and Kayden

The Destiny of Violet and Luke

The Probability of Violet and Luke

The Certainty of Violet and Luke

The Resolution of Callie and Kayden

Seth & Greyson

The Evermore of Callie and Kayden

Untitled (coming soon)

The Secret Series:

The Prelude of Ella and Micha

The Secret of Ella and Micha

The Forever of Ella and Micha

The Temptation of Lila and Ethan

The Ever After of Ella and Micha

Lila and Ethan: Forever and Always

Ella and Micha: Infinitely and Always

Untitled (coming soon)

The Shattered Promises Series:

Shattered Promises

Fractured Souls

Unbroken

Broken Visions

Scattered Ashes

Breaking Nova Series:

Breaking Nova

Saving Quinton

Delilah: The Making of Red

Nova and Quinton: No Regrets

Tristan: Finding Hope

Wreck Me

Ruin Me

The Fallen Star Series:

The Fallen Star

The Underworld

The Vision

The Promise

The Lost Soul

The Evanescence

The Mist of Stars (coming soon)

The Darkness Falls Series:

Darkness Falls

Darkness Breaks

Darkness Fades

The Death Collectors Series (NA and YA):

Ember X and Ember

Cinder X and Cinder

Spark X and Spark

Unbeautiful Series:

Unbeautiful

Untamed

Lexi Ashford:

Diary of Lexi Ashford

Diary of Lexi Ashford: The Deal

Untitled (coming soon)